R
the

REBECCA YORK

MILLS & BOON
Pure reading pleasure™

*First published in Great Britain 2009
by Harlequin Mills & Boon Limited,
Eton House, 18-24 Paradise Road, Richmond, Surrey TW9 1SR*

© Ruth Glick 2007

ISBN: 978 0 263 87304 7

46-0709

*Harlequin Mills & Boon policy is to use papers that are
natural, renewable and recyclable products and made from
wood grown in sustainable forests. The logging and
manufacturing processes conform to the legal environmental
regulations of the country of origin.*

*Printed and bound in Spain
by Litografia Rosés S.A., Barcelona*

They were Luke McMillan's dark eyes, the eyes that had given admiring looks. Yet at the same time, they belonged to someone else.

A man who was more assessing. More commanding. More dangerous than Luke McMillan had ever been. So was it Luke, or the warrior who'd taken up residence in his body?

She felt herself tremble in his arms as he lowered his mouth to hers. She tried to speak but his lips captured the sound. At the same time she forgot what she intended to say. Had she wanted to stop him, or let him know she liked what he was doing?

Fear and need warred within her. Desire won. She knew she wanted him as she'd never wanted anyone else in her life. The realisation was shocking. Was it proof that she'd lost her good sense…or was she simply helpless to resist the combination of the two men – one she knew and one she wanted to know?

Available in July 2009
from Mills & Boon® Intrigue

Return of the Warrior
by Rebecca York

Motive: Secret Baby
by Debra Webb

Scions: Insurrection
by Patrice Michelle

Killer Passion
by Sheri WhiteFeather

The New Deputy in Town
by BJ Daniels

Out of Uniform
by Catherine Mann

Around-the-Clock Protector
by Jan Hambright

Last Wolf Watching
by Rhyannon Byrd

ABOUT THE AUTHOR

Award-winning, bestselling novelist Ruth Glick, who writes as Rebecca York, has written more than one hundred books, including her popular 43 Light Street series for the Mills & Boon® Intrigue line. Ruth says she has the best job in the world. As well as authoring many works of fiction, Ruth has also written twelve cookbooks. Ruth and her husband, Norman, travel frequently, researching locales for her novels and searching out new dishes for her cookbooks.

Dear Reader,

I love writing stories where the hero and heroine fall in love against a background of danger and suspense. And I love throwing in a paranormal element – where they're also battling forces beyond the normal bounds of our everyday world.

Return of the Warrior is one of those stories. From the moment Luke McMillan opens the ancient box that arrived in a shipment of stolen antiques, he's in trouble. And so is Sidney Weston, the art expert unpacking the consignment. Sinister men will stop at nothing to acquire this object of power, which belongs to an ancient religious cult, the Moon Priests. They've been forgotten by modern society, but they're still around, protecting the interests of the human race.

Luke and Sidney are in for a shock. The Moon Priests have given the chest special protections. The spirit of an ancient warrior is locked inside, and when he comes roaring out, he enters Luke's body and forces him to protect the box. Of course, Luke must take Sidney with him, since her life is also at risk. Luke was an ordinary guy. Now he's become an extraordinary combination of his own personality and the warrior's. He's coping with this new reality and also his growing love for Sidney. So hang on for a wild ride.

*Rebecca York (*aka *Ruth Glick)*

Prologue

"Let's run through the drill again. The first rule is—do not hesitate to kill. The second rule—do not open the box under any circumstances."

Mr. Smith spoke quietly as he issued his final orders to the other two thieves.

Mr. Jones and Mr. Brown picked up their handguns from the bedside tables and checked the magazines. Then they returned to their seats on the hotel room sofa and chair and focused on their leader.

All three men were of medium height, their well-toned muscles giving them the look of bionic soldiers. All three had dark eyes and olive skin.

Their names were convenient fictions, of course, chosen to help them blend into the Baltimore urban landscape. None of them were American citizens, but each had identification to prove that he had been born in the States and resided here.

In reality, they would be in the country only long enough to steal the priceless antique box they had been hired to acquire. They would be leaving the hotel suite soon, and suppressed excitement thickened the air.

Excitement, not fear, Mr. Smith assured himself. They were too disciplined to let their nerves show. They would execute the mission without a hitch, and they would be rewarded handsomely with a million dollars each, deposited in Swiss bank accounts.

He refused to consider the alternative. Because failure meant death for the three of them.

They'd deplaned at BWI the week before and passed through customs and immigration without a snag. Initially they had been posing as European antique dealers on a buying trip to the United States. Once inside the country, they'd switched IDs.

They'd also acquired the weapons they needed, then gotten comfortable driving the narrow streets of Baltimore. It was an ugly city, but that was of little importance, since they'd be leaving soon.

They'd taken turns checking out the location of their target, watching the comings and goings at the front door, the garage and the loading dock.

But that was only part of their drill. Every day, they jogged for five miles around the Inner Harbor, then worked out at a downtown gym, keeping their bodies in shape so that they functioned like a well-oiled attack machine.

Mr. Smith looked at his watch. "Almost time."

He picked up a paper from the dresser and unfolded it. It showed a drawing of a wooden chest, about a foot long and eight inches across, whose entire surface was covered with ornate carvings of vines, flowers, animals and phases of the moon. They had studied it countless times.

"It's beautiful," Mr. Brown murmured.

"The power is more important than the beauty," Mr. Smith answered.

"Will we feel the power?" Mr. Jones asked in a hushed voice.

No one had asked that question previously, and Mr. Smith took it as a sign that nerves were finally breaking through their carefully cultivated calm.

"You may sense something," Smith answered, keeping his words slow and even to cover the inconvenient fact that he was just guessing at the answer. "The ancient magic has a seductive power, but there is no danger if the lid remains closed."

Mr. Jones nodded, apparently satisfied.

Smith folded the picture and put it in his pants pocket, then looked toward the bags sitting beside the door. The luggage was going in the car when they left the room, and the team would be ready to leave the city as soon as they pulled off the theft of the century.

Not at a bank or a museum but at a small import company called Peterbalm Associates, which was woefully ill-prepared for their visit.

Chapter One

Is this shipment of antiques stolen?

Sidney Weston kept the question locked behind her lips as she glanced from her boss, Carl Peterbalm, to the wooden packing crates that sat on the floor of her office.

Peterbalm was a short man in his mid-forties, with small, beady eyes, fleshy lips, and thinning hair. Not a very attractive package, especially accompanied by the garlic smell of his breath.

He was standing nearby, his arms folded across his ample middle, waiting for her to bring out more of the items he'd acquired from a French dealer who got his stock from God knew where. Wishing the crates weren't so deep, she leaned into one of the containers to get another antique, aware of Carl's hot gaze on her ass and legs.

On her worst days, she suspected that he'd hired her because he liked to show her off to clients and pretend they were having an affair.

As distasteful as that thought was, she needed the salary he provided, so she'd have to wait until she got another job before she went after him for sexual harassment.

She clutched the newspaper-wrapped object in her

hand, then ordered herself to relax as she carefully peeled off the paper to find a delicate Limoges pitcher, which she set beside the Louis XIV clock and solid silver altar candlestick that she'd already unwrapped.

She'd been working as a research assistant, secretary and gofer at Peterbalm Associates for eighteen months, and she longed to tell Mr. Grabby Hands to go to hell. Really, she wanted to open her own shop, where she'd have an appealing mixture of affordable collectibles and expensive antiques.

But for now, that was just a dream. She was still paying off the college loans that had allowed her to get a degree in fine arts at the University of Maryland.

When she turned, her breast brushed against his arm, which he'd positioned right where she would collide with him when she went back for more pieces from the shipment.

"Sorry," he said, the insecurity dripping from his voice.

Biting back a sharp retort, she reached into the carton and brought out another antique. Through the paper she felt a rectangular object. With the wrapping still on, she couldn't see the thing, but she felt the hairs on the backs of her arms stand up. Whatever she was holding, she suddenly wanted to put it back into the shipping container.

Instead, she clenched her teeth and started to unwrap it. As she pulled away the paper, she saw a wooden box with elaborate carvings of vines, flowers, animals and moons. When her hand touched the wood, her fingers tingled. Setting the box down abruptly on the table, she took a couple of steps back. Even from a few feet away, the thing seemed to exude a kind of invisible power that she had never felt before.

Behind her, Carl sucked in a sharp breath. Did he feel something too?

"What?" she asked.

He waited a beat before saying, "I just remembered that I'm late for an appointment." He swept his arm toward the wooden crates. "I want you to finish unpacking the shipment today, and enter everything in the computer file."

She flicked her eyes toward the time stamp at the bottom of her computer screen. It was already four in the afternoon. To finish on time, she'd have to work overtime, and she knew from past experience that Carl Peterbalm was unlikely to pay her for the extra hours.

"That may take awhile," she murmured.

"You can clock in an extra hour," he said.

Big whoop.

"Thank you," she answered.

When he left the room and marched down the hall, Sidney breathed out a little sigh.

She knew Carl was still trying to prove to his father that he could do better on his own than by joining the family business. No doubt he'd ordered this shipment from some under-the-table source, and now he'd left her with the result.

Still, she could work a lot faster without him breathing down her neck.

She glanced at the clock again. At this hour, the rest of the staff had probably had already gone home, which added to her uneasy feeling.

Ordering herself to settle down, she got up and locked the door. Then she returned to inventory the shipment.

It wasn't going to be a simple task. In addition to listing each item, she also had to write a description, which might require some research on the Web or in the reference books that lined the shelves above the computer table.

She unwrapped a couple more pieces from the shipment, setting them on the table. Then, almost against her own will, her hand was drawn back to the wooden box. When she touched it, she felt the same tingling sensation she'd experienced before, as though it had an electric current running through it.

No, it was more than that. Somehow she felt the tingling inside her head. As if it was getting into her mind.

Stop it, she ordered. You're letting your imagination run away with you.

Still, she knew the chest had to be something extraordinary.

And it had come in a cut-rate shipment from France? Not likely.

She stroked her finger over the carved surface that had become nicked and scarred over the years, then gently traced the curve of a three-quarter moon before picking up the box and holding it near her ear. Did she detect a faint buzzing, or was it her imagination? She shook the box and heard a faint rattling sound, like someone had locked a piece of plastic inside.

What was in there anyway? And how did you open it? As far as she could see, it had no obvious lid. It must be like one of those Oriental puzzle boxes where you had to press a sequence of places on the surface to make panels slide to one side or the other.

She fiddled with the chest for a few minutes, but she couldn't locate any hidden panels.

Maybe she was wrong. Maybe whoever had made the thing had intended it to just be a paperweight.

She didn't believe that, but perhaps she could get some help from an expert. She started to reach for the phone, then drew her hand back. Carl was a real cheapskate who had a limited calling plan and monitored the phone records. He'd complain if she made a personal call on his dime. So she dug her cell phone out of her purse, then dialed Sabrina Cassidy.

Sabrina ran the lobby shop at 43 Light Street, a downtown office building with a close-knit community of friends and coworkers.

Her store carried the usual sundries that people who worked in the building might need, but she also had a charming selection of antiques and gift items.

Sidney had done an internship with her during her senior year at Maryland, and they'd become good friends. Through Sabrina she'd also met a lot of the other people from the Light Street address.

Sabrina answered on the second ring. "Lobby Shop."

"I'm glad I reached you."

"Sidney! You sound…upset. What's wrong? Do you have a problem?"

"Well, I'm stuck at the office with a big shipment of antiques from France. I've got to write up an inventory, and I was hoping you could tell me something about one of the pieces."

"What have you got?

"A carved box. It's very old, and it looks like it came from India or maybe China."

In as much detail as possible, she described the box, leaving out the part about the electric sensation, because she felt embarrassed to admit her strange reaction.

"And there's no obvious way to open it?" Sabrina asked.

"No."

Her friend was silent for a moment. "I…"

"What?"

"From your description, it might be associated with an ancient religious cult."

"What cult?"

"The Moon Priests. They flourished on the Indian subcontinent almost two thousand years ago. Also in mainland Greece. At one time they were a powerful force in the world."

"But not now?"

"I thought they died out."

Sidney felt a shiver travel over her skin. She'd thought the box was old. It sounded like her estimate was off by a millennium.

"The Moon Priests were reputed to have magical— or mystical—powers."

The comment made the hairs on her arm stir again. To banish the feeling, she laughed. "Well, a lot of religions make that claim. You could go back to Moses and the burning bush."

"Right." Sabrina cleared her throat. "I'd like to see the box."

Sidney thought about the request. She was sure that Carl wouldn't like someone else looking at his shipment. But Carl wasn't here now.

"Can you come tonight?"

"I wish I could, but Dan is taking me to dinner. We've been trying to find the time to get together for weeks."

Sabrina had met her husband when she was a murder suspect and he was a State's Attorney. Since then, he'd given up his government job and gone to work for the

Light Street Foundation, helping people who couldn't afford the usual legal fees.

"What about early tomorrow morning, before my boss gets in?"

"Thanks. I'd like that."

Knowing that she'd better get to work if she didn't want to spend the night at the office, Sidney ended the call, then turned back to the shipment.

She understood herself pretty well, and she knew that filling a computer file with information would make her feel better. So she reached for the Limoges pitcher. She'd studied French china in one of her senior classes, and she could describe and date the piece without using a reference book.

She'd just entered the information when the screen and the cursor froze.

"Lord, no!" she muttered as she tried to move the cursor. When nothing happened, she was forced to press the Control-Alt-Delete keys. A box came up on the left side of the screen, telling her that the program was not responding and she would lose all data she'd entered if she chose to terminate the program.

Since she'd only recorded one item, maybe the best thing to do was to start over. She pressed the cancel keys again, but instead of just losing the program, the computer shut itself off.

Panic shot through her. "Not now," she pleaded as she tried to reboot.

But the machine wouldn't come back on.

With an unsteady hand, she reached for the Rolodex on her desk. She used her cell phone to dial Luke McMillan, the guy who had sold Carl the desktop and still serviced it. As she listened to it ring, she murmured a little prayer under her breath. "Please, God. Please, let him answer," she repeated over and over. On the fifth ring, she heard his voice.

"Thank you God," she breathed.

He laughed. "I sound that good?"

"Luke, I need you. I'm in the middle of an inventory project, and my computer's crapped out."

"Okay. I just finished a job downtown, and I'm in my car. I'll be there in fifteen minutes."

"I owe you."

He paused for a moment, then asked, "What?"

"Get me up and running again, and we'll talk about it," she said. In truth, she was thinking that maybe this would be the push Luke needed to ask her out. He was so damn cute with his shaggy dark hair and that sexy cleft in his chin. But he'd always struck her as a study in contrasts. He was so confident when it came to his job and so shy around her.

She hated to admit how much she liked him, even to herself.

Still, she couldn't squelch a feeling of anticipation as she got up and unlocked the door that she'd locked a few minutes ago. While she was up, she made a quick trip to the ladies' room where she used the facilities, then combed her blond hair and put on some fresh lipstick.

"Going out on a date?" Betty Custer asked as she came out of the other stall. Betty worked down the hall for a trucking company. A petite redhead, she was a few years older than Sidney, and they'd gotten to know each other.

"I wish," Sidney answered. "Carl has me stuck here for the evening."

"You're not putting on lipstick for Carl, are you?" Betty asked as she washed her hands.

Sidney flushed. "Luke McMillan is coming by."

When Sidney had casually mentioned Luke before, Betty had revealed that she'd gone to school with him. So Sidney had pressed her for information and found out a lot about him. Luke hadn't been shy around the girls in school. Sidney was sure he liked her, so why did he keep hanging back?

"Did he finally ask you out?" Betty asked.

Sidney inspected her appearance in the mirror. Not too bad for a woman who'd been at work all day. "No, but maybe I can push him over the edge tonight."

"Good luck."

"Thanks."

LUKE MCMILLAN PRESSED DOWN on the accelerator, and the sporty little Beemer shot forward.

The bad boy of Highlandtown High in a BMW. He still grinned when he thought about it.

The car had been a mess when he'd taken it in payment for a major network installation that a client couldn't pay for. The guy had thought he was pulling a fast one, but Luke had stripped down the engine in his garage and put it back together, turning it into a smooth-running dream of a machine. A friend who owned a body shop had handled the exterior work, and Luke had buffed up the classic leather seats.

He was good with his hands. And good at striking deals. So here he was riding around in a set of wheels that would make his grandma drop her false teeth.

He looked down at the dark T-shirt, jeans and low

boots he was wearing. Passable, but not great. Could he get Sidney to go out with him later, after he fixed her computer?

His hands tightened on the wheel, and he made an effort to relax his hold.

He'd met Sidney six months ago when Carl Peterbalm had revamped his computer system. The importer had wanted to cut costs by using reconditioned units, and Luke had given him the best value for the money. But that didn't mean the hardware was top of the line.

As he headed for the building in the warehouse district next to Greektown where Peterbalm had his import business, he thought about Sidney.

She was the most memorable thing about his dealings with Peterbalm. And the cheapskate had gotten better service than he should have expected because Luke had no problem going back there to visit his assistant.

She was his dream girl. He loved the way her chin-length blond hair swung around her face when she turned her head. The big blue eyes he could drown in. The mouth he longed to kiss. And the cute little figure that filled out a sweater and a pair of slacks so nicely.

She'd always been friendly when he'd installed the equipment and come back to the office to service it.

But maybe she was just being polite. Why would she be interested in a guy who grew up in Highlandtown, had barely made it through high school, and grubbed around with computers? Sure he had worked hard to make something of himself. But he had no polish, while she was a college graduate who knew all about art and antiques.

Still, he could help her out tonight. And maybe she'd like to go out for a beer after she got off work.

He made a harsh sound as he pulled into the building's garage and cut the engine. Sure, a woman like her would love to be seen in the working-class bars he frequented.

SIDNEY PACED BACK AND forth as she waited for Luke to arrive, glancing occasionally at the carved chest that still sat on the table with the other antiques. It was just a box, for Lord's sake. But the damn thing made her nervous. She couldn't help thinking that it was going to bring her bad luck. More than anything she wanted to get it out of the office, but she couldn't just throw it away. Carl had already seen it.

What was she thinking? Throw away a valuable antique? Of course not.

Instead of focusing on the chest, she turned her thoughts back to Luke McMillan. By her standards, he was a rough around the edges kind of guy. Not like the young businessmen or lawyers she'd met at church. But she'd been attracted to him from the first time they'd met.

The problem was, she didn't know how to get anything going with him. She had the feeling he didn't think he met her standards. And perhaps when she'd been in college and dating a bunch of preppy guys, that would have been true. Now that she'd been working for a couple of years, she understood what an achievement it was that he'd established his own business and kept it going.

That's what she wanted for herself. Maybe he could even give her some pointers, if he'd loosen up and talk to her.

She thought back over their phone conversation. He'd

been flirting with her. Maybe they could keep the banter going in person.

A noise at the door made her go rigid. When she whirled around, she saw Luke and breathed out a sigh.

"That was fast. Thanks for coming."

"For you, anything." A cocky smile flashed across his face as he strode into the room, glancing from the computer to her and back again. "So what's going on with this puppy?" he asked.

"It froze and now it won't boot." As she answered, she realized that it was after hours, and they were alone in the office together. At her invitation.

Was he thinking about that, too?

He went over and fiddled with the keyboard and got the same non-response that she had.

When his cell phone rang, he pulled it out and checked the number.

"Who's that?" she asked.

"A client."

"And you're not going to respond?"

"I'm busy."

He put the phone down on the desk, then turned the machine around, fiddling with some of the attachments.

"I see what's wrong," he said.

"Thank God. What?"

"The plug at the computer end of the power cord is loose. It happens sometimes, when the machine gets moved around."

"I don't remember doing that."

"Does Carl ever work in here?"

"Yes."

"Okay. Well, the important point is that I think I've

solved the problem." Opening the briefcase he'd brought along, he shuffled through the contents, then triumphantly pulled out a cord.

"Here's an early birthday present."

"You know when my birthday is?"

"Just a figure of speech." Turning away from her, he swapped the new cord for the one that had been attached to the machine.

So, had he been snooping in the computer files and looked at her personal information? Did he know her birthday was next week? She might have asked, but the rigid lines of his shoulders warned her not to question him.

Still with his back to her, he pressed the power button, and the screen lit up.

Profound relief washed over her. "Thank you so much. You saved my life," she said.

He turned and looked up at her. "So do you want to take a dinner break? With me."

She felt her chest tighten. He'd finally made a move and she couldn't go with him. Not tonight.

"Luke, I'd like to. But I have to get this inventory done before tomorrow morning. That's why I was working late in the first place."

"Yeah."

"I'm not trying to make excuses. I'd love to go out with you. But I can't tonight."

"What do you have to do?"

She waved her hand toward the crates. "Unpack a boatload of stuff and record everything."

He shifted his weight from one foot to the other. "What if I helped with the unpacking?"

"Would you?"

"Sure." He walked toward the cases, then stopped at the table where she'd set the objects she'd already removed. Somehow she'd known that he was going to go right to the carved wooden box.

Picking it up, he turned it over in his hands. "What's this?"

"A friend of mine says it's from an old religious cult. The Moon Priests."

"Never heard of them." He began moving his fingers over the sides of the chest. When she'd done it, she'd gotten absolutely no results, but when Luke pressed the lower right side of the box, a panel sprang back.

"Hey!" he exclaimed, then propped his hips against the table as he turned the box, holding it up to the light and looking at the design. Then he pressed a flower on the left side. Again, a panel opened, and she felt a jolt of alarm.

"Don't."

He looked up and then back at the chest. "I'm not going to break it."

"That's not what I'm worried about."

"What, then?"

"Put it down."

"In a minute. I think it's interesting."

"And I think it's dangerous." Even as she said it, she felt silly. How could an antique be dangerous?

"Maybe they hid some jewels inside." He shook it, listening to the faint sound. "Let me find out what's in here. I'm good with my hands. And careful with delicate things." His gaze flicked from the box to her. He held her eyes for just a moment, then went back to the task.

Now she knew he was flirting.

Any other time, she would have enjoyed the give and take, but this evening she was desperate to stop him. She considered crossing the space between them and snatching the damn thing out of his hand. Instead, she tried another approach. "You remember that chest in the *Raiders of the Lost Ark*?"

"What about it?"

"When the Nazis opened it, something bad happened to them."

"This isn't the lost ark."

"It is from an ancient religion."

"And?"

"And it's giving me the creeps."

He laughed.

"Don't make fun of me. I've had a bad feeling about that thing ever since I unwrapped it. And Carl did too. I think that's why he left."

"Um hum." He ignored the warning and kept working on the box. More panels opened, and then the top sprang up.

As Sidney watched in horror, a white mist blasted out of the box like it had been fired from a cannon and struck Luke in the face.

Chapter Two

Sidney gasped.

The whole room seemed to go cold as the white vapor enveloped Luke. He made a strangled sound and staggered back, the fingers of his right hand clamped around the chest. With his free hand, he scrabbled at the edge of the table as he tried to steady himself.

His face had turned pale as death, and a shudder raced across his skin.

"What the hell…" The sentence ended in a wheeze as he tried and failed to fill his lungs.

While Sidney watched in horror, his body began to jerk, like someone having a grand mal seizure. But she was sure it wasn't because he had any illness. It was from the white mist.

"Luke!" she screamed as he toppled forward, knocking the pitcher off the table when he fell.

The delicate china shattered, and Luke's body continued to shake as he hit the floor.

"Oh Lord."

Sidney dropped to her knees, quickly pushing the shards of porcelain out of the way as she knelt beside Luke.

His eyes were closed, and his body was still shaking, his muscles twitching and contracting.

Finally, the quaking stopped, and she whispered a silent prayer.

He lay deathly still, his face pale as salt and his breathing shallow. But at least he *was* breathing. When she pressed her fingers to the artery in his neck, she felt his pulse beating and also the warmth of his skin.

"Luke?"

He didn't answer. What had that awful white mist from the box done to him? Was it some kind of poison? It couldn't be a virus or a bacteria, could it? Not and hit him that fast, she told herself.

But she couldn't help wondering if she was going to start gasping, then go unconscious.

"Luke?" she said again. She shook his shoulder gently, but he didn't move. She glanced toward the phone on the table, thinking she should call 911. He needed medical help—help she couldn't provide.

But when she started to get up, his hand shot out and captured her wrist, holding her in an iron grip.

Her gaze shot to his face as his eyes blinked open and focused on her. They were Luke McMillan's dark eyes, the eyes that had given her an admiring look when he'd first come strolling into the office. Yet, at the same time they belonged to someone else. A man who was more assessing. More commanding. More dangerous than Luke McMillan had ever been.

That was impossible. But she couldn't shake the conviction that the man clamping her wrist in his hand had changed in some fundamental way when that mist had hit him.

He was staring at her mouth with an open lust that Luke would never have let her see. Or had she been fooling herself about him all along? Was he really a lot less civilized than she'd assumed?

His lips moved, and he said a bunch of syllables that made no sense to her. It was like he was suddenly speaking in a language she couldn't understand.

"What?"

He didn't reply.

When she tried to pull away, he kept his iron grip on her wrist, but his gaze had turned inward, and it looked like he was listening to some voice she couldn't hear.

Then his lips moved again. This time, he murmured her name, although the accent was strange, as though he had spoken some other language all his life.

"Sidney."

"You recognize me?"

"Yes. You were with him when he opened the box. He was thinking about how much he wanted to make love to you." Again, his accent was unfamiliar.

"What do you mean—him? It was you," she said in a voice she couldn't keep steady.

"It was me," he said slowly, apparently considering the statement. Then his gaze focused on her again.

"You. Luke McMillan."

"Luke McMillan?" he mused. "A strong name. Good."

Then she saw him switch his attention back to her. "You're lovely," he said, his tone deep and rough.

"I have to call 911. You need to go to the hospital."

His eyes turned fierce. "No."

Before she could move, he reached up with his free hand and drew her down against the hard wall of his chest.

She managed to say, "Don't," before he cupped his hand around the back of her head and brought her lips to his.

His mouth moved under hers, hungry and demanding, like a man who had been denied all pleasure for a thousand years or more. Or maybe a man released from prison and desperate for the sensations of the world.

He changed the pressure of his lips, subtly softening the kiss, and that was sexier than his previous assault.

As he devoured her mouth, his hands were busy, sliding down her back, molding her body to his. Even as heat roared through her veins, somewhere in her mind, she was shocked—by her own behavior and by his.

This was wrong! Luke had just gotten hurt. And she shouldn't be draped on top of him making out.

If this *was* Luke.

A dart of fear stabbed her as that notion lodged in her brain again. This had to be Luke. Who else could it be?

The frantic thought evaporated as soon as it had formed. She was too busy responding to the sexy man who clasped her in his arms.

When he realized she wasn't going to pull away, he drew her lower lip into his mouth, sucking and nibbling. He was good at what he was doing, and she heard a small murmur of arousal rise in her throat.

He seemed to drink in the sound as he silently asked her to open for him. She did, thrilling to the stroke of his tongue against hers. As he deepened the kiss, he slid her body fully on top of his, then swept his fingers across her back, pulling out the hem of her blouse. His hand slipped inside and stroked her skin, large and warm and firm against her heated flesh. He made a needy sound deep in his throat.

She answered in kind as he cupped her bottom through the fabric of her slacks, pressing her against his erection.

He was ready to make love to her. And she responded with a surge of arousal.

"Hold me," he said in a gritty voice.

She did as he asked, clutching his broad shoulders as he reversed their positions, coming down on top of her, then raising up on his hands so that he could look into her dazed eyes.

It felt like the world had vanished. Only the two of them existed in a bubble of supercharged sexuality.

For months she had been attracted to Luke McMillan, had wondered what it would be like to make love with him. Well, now she was finding out. In the past few moments he had turned into the most exciting man she had ever met.

She knew without doubt that he would have her naked soon, and then he would join his body with hers right here on the floor of her office.

He moved, and his boot scraped the floor, hitting a piece of the pitcher that he'd pulled off the table when he fell.

"What was that?" he asked.

"The pitcher. You pushed it off the table when you went down."

He uttered something that might have been a curse in that foreign language he'd used before. Then he levered himself off of her, stood and helped her to her feet. "We are in danger."

"What danger?"

"From the thieves who want the box."

The answer made no sense to her, yet she heard the absolute conviction in his voice.

He flexed his muscles, moving his arms and legs like a man stretching after a long night's sleep.

Again he seemed to be paying attention to some voice she couldn't hear.

"Who are you listening to?" she asked.

"Luke McMillan."

"You are Luke McMillan," she snapped.

"Yes. And also I am Zabastian, the guardian of the box."

"Oh come on." Even as she spoke, she was wondering if he'd seriously damaged his brain when he'd hit the floor. Or had she damaged hers? He'd hurt himself, and she'd come down on top of him, her lips fused to his in a heated kiss.

She could say that he'd pulled her down. But she hadn't objected. And he certainly hadn't been behaving like the Luke McMillan she knew. That guy was shy—at least with her.

This man was anything but shy. He was commanding. He knew what he wanted, and he knew how to get it.

He interrupted her thoughts with another of his cryptic comments.

"Luke is still here. But he is not in control. He cannot be. Not now."

"What are you talking about? Why do you sound so…stilted?"

Ignoring her, he reached down to scoop the box off the floor. "How did you come by this?"

"It arrived in a shipment of antiques from France."

"I do not understand the reference," he said, standing

quietly again. Then his expression cleared. "Luke has told me about France. The Coneheads are from France."

She laughed. "Is that what he thought of first? There are a few other things—like Bordeaux wine, onion soup and champagne."

"We will discuss France later. We must leave before the thieves arrive."

He turned toward the door, but stopped him.

"Wait a minute. You're not going anywhere until you explain who you are, if you're not Luke."

"I already told you my name. I am Zabastian, a warrior whose spirit was trapped in the box."

Okay. She'd play along, try to figure out his game. "Like a genie in a bottle?" she asked sweetly.

"I have heard of that. The genie grants wishes?"

"Yes."

"I do not," he said firmly.

She stared at him. Maybe he wasn't playing games. Maybe he was afflicted with a multiple personality disorder or something, and he'd hid it well until he hit his head.

"Luke is still in your body?" she asked carefully.

"Yes."

"Let me talk to him."

His face contorted. "We do not have time for a conversation now. We are in danger. We must leave this place."

Her exasperation bubbled over. "Let me talk to Luke!"

LUKE OPENED HIS MOUTH, then closed it again. He wanted to speak, but apparently the guy who had taken over his body wasn't going to let him.

She needs to know what's going on, he said inside his mind, hearing the words echo internally.

Later, Zabastian answered.

I'll kill you later, Luke growled.

You'll kill yourself, then, monkey brain.

Wait a minute. You don't have to insult me.

Then think logically.

Luke balled his free hand into a fist—the one that wasn't clutching the haunted box.

He'd been strangely drawn to the damn thing, as if some magical force was tugging on him, goading him to try and solve the puzzle. Too bad he hadn't kept his hands to himself when Sidney had warned him to leave it alone.

He'd thought he was so clever when he'd started working the sliding panels. Once he'd gotten the first one, his fingers had moved over the carved design on the sides as fast as the wind.

He'd slid hidden panels and pressed levers as if somebody else was directing his movements. And he was pretty sure that was true. It seemed that the guy inside the chest—the spirit of some kind of ancient warrior—had connected with Luke's mind, even when he was still trapped inside the chest.

He'd wanted Luke to let him out. When the lid had popped open, the essence of the warrior had come pouring out, like steam from a valve under pressure. The living mist of the man's spirit had enveloped Luke, knocking him to the floor with the force of the invasion and knocking him unconscious.

When he'd awakened, Sidney had been kneeling over him. He'd been trying to speak to her when Zabastian had taken over.

Apparently the guy hadn't had a woman in over three hundred years, and he'd been ready to force himself on Sidney right there on the floor.

I did not force myself, an outraged voice inside his head answered. *She wanted me.*

She thought it was me!

And she liked what we were doing.

Luke had liked it too. He'd been trying to get somewhere with Sidney for six months. In minutes Zabastian had cut right to the chase.

Too bad his foot had hit that pitcher.

Later!

Get the hell out of my head.

You need me.

To prove the point, a sound in the doorway made his head snap up.

Two short olive-complected men dressed in business suits charged through the door. Each of them held a gun in his hand—pointed at him and Sidney.

The Poisoned Ones.

Who?

The men who have come to take the box. They will kill you and the woman to acquire it.

Luke swore under his breath, knowing that he and Sidney didn't have a chance of survival. Not with the fruitcake named Zabastian running the show.

I know how to fight! Better than you, the warrior's voice said inside his head.

But not these guys. And you don't even know how my body works.

True.

The silent messages flickered with lightning speed.

And you've never seen a gun, right? Luke pressed.

He felt the warrior search his mind. *I have seen them. Other times when I awoke. A weapon that shoots deadly projectiles.*

Yeah, well, they've gotten more sophisticated in the last few hundred years.

We must cooperate to defeat these dung flies.

Could they? It was going to be difficult, but maybe that was their only chance.

The whole conversation had flashed back and forth between them in nanoseconds, since it was more like an internal thought process than speech. And Luke had never taken his attention away from the men with the guns.

"Give me the box," one of them ordered.

"No."

The man raised his weapon, preparing to take what he had come for.

Moving like a streak of light, Luke thrust the box into Sidney's hands and shoved her to the side as he charged the one who had spoken.

He took them by surprise, because they weren't expecting resistance. He kicked upward with his foot, catching the man in the gun hand.

The would-be attacker screamed and dropped the weapon.

Luke whirled, using what he knew must be some kind of martial art. He couldn't name the moves he was making, but they were effective. He took down the other guy, then jabbed the first one in the stomach with his elbow. From his peripheral vision, he saw Sidney bring down an ornate metal candlestick on the head of the man who was trying to get up, knocking him to the ground in a heap.

The first one he'd kicked had pulled out another gun, holding it in his left hand. Before he could bring it into firing position, Luke chopped down on his wrist, eliciting a satisfying scream.

He turned to Sidney. "Give me the box."

She complied, and he tucked it firmly under his arm. "Come on. We've got to get out of here."

The second man was climbing to his feet. Luke kicked him down again, then ducked around him and made for the door, pulling Sidney behind him.

"Where are the stairs?"

Sidney pointed halfway down the hallway.

As they ran down the corridor, a woman stepped out of another office, her face tense.

"What was that?"

"A robbery. Get out of the hall," Luke shouted, then stared at the woman. He knew her. It was Betty Custer, and she had gone to school with him.

She ducked back into her office and asked in a hoarse whisper, "Should I call the police?"

"No. Just stay out of sight. Hide."

They rushed past.

"Why not call the police?" Sidney gasped out.

"The men who tried to steal the box won't let themselves be captured. People will die."

"Who are they?"

"I told you. The Poisoned Ones. They came to steal the box, to acquire its power. They will risk everything to win the prize. Stop asking questions," he said as they reached the stairs. He yanked open the door and ushered Sidney inside.

He could feel Zabastian inside him. It was a strange sensation—a combination of power and helplessness. The warrior was still getting his bearings, and he had let Luke take charge, now that the fight was over. But what he was telling Sidney about the Poisoned Ones came straight from the warrior.

"Stay in the background," he muttered under his breath.

"What?" Sidney asked.

He felt heat stain his cheeks as he considered what she must be thinking. "I'm not talking to you."

"Then who?"

"Zabastian. You remember him?" he asked as they ran down a flight of stairs.

"Luke, have you gotten…psychiatric treatment?" she puffed out as they ran.

"I don't need a shrink."

She shot him a sidewise look that told him she was planning to get away from him as soon as she could.

Well, he couldn't allow that. Because if the attackers didn't get the chest, they'd come looking for her.

"What? You think those guys are my drug dealers, or maybe my bookies, come to take me out for not paying my bills?

"I don't know who they are."

"They're after the box. Like they told you."

She made a strangled sound. Apparently it was too difficult to breathe and keep asking questions.

They reached the garage level of the building, and he pulled open the door. Without waiting to find out what was on the other side, he charged through.

His mistake.

"Stop!" a voice called, and he knew in that moment that the other two men had left a cohort in the garage, just in case.

The grating voice was followed by a barrage of bullets.

Luke had already pulled Sidney behind a rectangular pillar. Bullets struck it, chipping pieces of cement.

The angle was shifting. While they'd been striking the front of the column, now they were moving to the side.

"Down," he whispered. "Move behind the cars. Mine's the silver BMW."

She looked around. "Where?"

"Halfway down the row along this wall."

He reached into his pocket and handed her the key. "Get in. Drive toward the door."

"It's locked!"

"You have an opener in your car?"

"Yes. But it's on the other side of the garage, and we can't get to it."

"Is there a release at the door?"

"I think so."

"I'll get to the door and open it."

She gave him a panicked look.

"Go!"

She ducked low, moving along the wall, following his directions, and he gave her points for not arguing. He couldn't help wondering if he'd put her in worse danger.

The garage was half empty and deathly quiet, and he'd like to know where the gunman had disappeared.

Straining his ears, he tried to figure out where the guy was hiding. But he heard and saw nothing.

Praying that Sidney made it to his car in one piece, he crawled awkwardly to the exit gate with the box under his arm, using the remaining cars as cover and hoping the gunman didn't spot him.

But as he moved toward his goal, a wave of dizziness overtook him, and he saw black spots in front of his eyes. Even as he fought to hold on to consciousness, he felt it slipping from his grasp.

Panic tightened his throat.

"No," he ordered himself. "Not now."

But working with another person inside his head was taking its toll. Luke stopped, pressing his shoulder against a car bumper, feeling like he was hanging onto awareness by his fingernails. If he passed out, he was dead. And so was Sidney.

And the box is lost, the warrior growled inside his skull.

Right, the all-important box. That's what got us into this damn mess.

The warrior didn't respond to the sarcasm. But as Luke wavered on the cold cement floor, he felt his breathing change. It became slower and deeper, and he knew the warrior was using some kind of calming technique on his mind and body. It helped. After a minute, the black spots went away, and Luke felt like he could function again.

"Thanks," he muttered as he started crawling again toward the front of the garage where a metal gate closed off the entrance. Luckily there was a car parked nearby, which gave him some cover. But when he reached for the red button that opened the door, the gunman spotted him and started shooting.

Shots rang out from the other end of the garage, too,

and he realized that at least one of the men they'd disabled upstairs had made it down here.

He ducked behind the car as the metal gate began to slowly open. But he didn't like his chances of getting into the BMW with two men catching him in the crossfire. Worse, he'd draw that fire toward Sidney.

Just as he was trying to figure out his next move, he heard an engine rev.

The BMW shot out of its parking slot, then whipped into forward gear and came barreling toward the gate— which was still not open enough for the car to exit.

His heart leaped into his throat when he heard bullets hit the back fender.

Chapter Three

Sidney ducked low to make herself as small a target as possible. Her hands fused to the wheel, she screeched to a halt in front of the gate that Luke had opened.

"Get in!" she screamed.

Luke bent at the waist, running around the front of the car and through the car door she'd thrown open.

She heard a man shout something in a language she didn't understand.

Her first thought was that it must be Arabic. Then she decided it had an Asian cadence. Or maybe Indian.

As Luke slammed the door closed, she was already lurching away, picking up speed as she cleared the gate, then slammed up the ramp to the street.

"They stopped shooting!" she shouted.

"The one from upstairs warned the shooter not to hit the box."

"Our lucky break."

"Yeah, they'll kill us if they catch up."

Sidney absorbed that with a grimace.

It was fully dark now, and she reached for the lever that turned on the headlights.

"Leave them off," Luke shouted as she made a quick left turn, then sped to the end of the block.

She didn't like driving in the dark with no lights, but she understood why it was important. And at least she didn't have to worry about much traffic on the streets around the warehouses.

BEFORE THE SILVER CAR was up the ramp, Smith, Jones and Brown sprinted for their rental car, and jumped in. Jones was driving, and he headed for the garage door, trying to catch up with the fleeing car.

Although the gate was already closing, he thought he could make it underneath before it was too late. But he had to slam on his brakes at the last minute when the gap became too small for their car to exit.

Smith cursed. "Get out," he said to Brown. "Open it again. Hurry. We've got to catch up with them."

Brown sprinted for the door opener and pressed the switch. As the door began to ascend again, he dashed back to the car. But by the time they emerged from the garage, the street was empty.

Smith cursed again.

"They can't have gotten far," Brown muttered.

Jones scanned the street. "I think they kept their lights off. Which way should I go?"

"If I'd been them, I would have turned right," Smith said.

Jones nodded, then made a right turn, speeding down the darkened street, as all of them watched for the little silver car. But it seemed to have vanished.

After several minutes, Jones admitted defeat and began driving more slowly. He didn't think he was going to find the couple right away. But they would keep trying.

"Now what?" Brown asked.

"We have to figure out where the man and the woman would go. Then kill them and take the box."

"The woman was an office worker," Smith said.

"Yes."

"But what about the man?"

"He was an office worker, too," Jones answered.

"I'm not so sure," Smith objected. "He showed martial training."

Both of his companions turned to him. "So who was he? And what was he doing there?" Brown asked.

Smith didn't answer directly. "You have read the accounts. Over the years, others have tried to steal the box, and they have ended up dead."

"They were incompetent," Jones answered.

"All of them?" Brown asked in a sharp voice.

"By definition. They failed."

"The question is why. What if the box has special protections?" Brown asked.

Jones and Smith stared at him. "Explain your thinking," Smith demanded.

"Did you see the eyes of the man?"

Jones swallowed. "What about them?"

"I think you know," Brown answered, his voice soft and even.

"What do I know?" Smith snapped. He had been thinking the worst, but he wasn't going to be the one to say it.

"There was a spirit in the box. He emerged when he sensed danger."

"Nonsense," Smith answered, but his voice no longer held the same conviction. "If he emerged, how did he acquire a body?"

"He took the body of that man," Brown said. He fixed Smith with a sharp look. "We may not survive this attempt at theft."

Smith glared at him, but fear jolted through him. They had contracted with powerful forces to steal the box, confident they had the skill and the training to recover the object of power. Now it appeared that they had not been told the whole story.

"We could just disappear," Brown said softly.

"No. They would track us down," Smith said. He didn't say who "they" were. Each of them knew.

"We must see this through," Smith added, keeping his private doubts to himself. He made his voice sharp. "We will surely not survive if you give up so easily."

He reached into his pocket and pulled out some sheets of paper. "We've lost them for now, but I have addresses from the office files. The woman is the assistant of Carl Peterbalm, and I know where she lives. They may go to her dwelling. And if they do," he said with a hard finality in his voice, "we will find them and kill them."

SIDNEY WAS FAMILIAR WITH this area because she'd had to take several different streets going to and from work when road repair crews had blocked her usual route.

Luke was looking over his shoulder. "There's a car behind you. It could be them."

"Not to worry," she answered, speeding up and weaving down one street, then another. She took another corner at a fast clip, then barreled down an alley into Greektown. With the quick maneuvers, she lost the car behind them and kept going.

Finally, she came to a street with a fair amount of traffic.

"All right to turn on the lights?"

"I guess you'd better."

She drove along a broad avenue and turned onto one of the side streets where she found a parking place. After maneuvering into the space, she turned to Luke. The interior of the car was dark, but she could see his tense features in the glow from a street lamp several yards down the block.

"They shot your car," she murmured.

"Yeah, it's going to need some body work. I have a friend who can take care of it for me. But I hope it's not like going to the doctor, and you have to explain why you got shot."

Her mind raced back over the frantic scene in the garage. "You said one of the men from upstairs told them to stop shooting."

"Yes."

"So you understood that language."

"Zabastian does."

"Zabastian. Oh sure. Why don't you tell me what's really going on."

"The box belongs to a religious group. They call themselves the Way of the Moon. Or simply, the Moon Priests."

Sabrina had mentioned an ancient moon cult, so that rang true. But how would Luke know about it? She pushed that question aside and tipped her head to the side, staring at him. "Why don't you give the box to those men and be done with it?"

"It does not belong to them. They want the power of the box for…" He paused and thought about it. "I do not know for who sent them."

"I thought the box was from an ancient cult. Are you saying it still has power?"

"The Way of the Moon is very ancient. They are still active in the world, and they still have enormous power. And so does the box."

"What is the power?"

"That is not for you to know."

"Well, thanks. I can get shot at trying to save the damn thing, but I can't know why."

His eyes turned fierce, and she realized she was talking directly to Zabastian, not Luke. "You must accept what I tell you."

She swallowed. "It's a difficult story to credit." Before he could object, she went on quickly. "What does the box have to do with us?"

"I was charged with the duty of protecting it."

"You? Luke or Zabastian?"

He gave her a long look. "I think you are smart enough to figure it out," he answered.

She held his gaze. "If what you're saying is true, then you're using Luke McMillan. Without his permission."

His face contorted, and she would have sworn that Luke was in there, that he was trying to say something to her. But this other man—the man she didn't know—had taken control of the conversation.

She waited with her stomach muscles clenched. And her assumption was confirmed when Zabastian said, "The box must be restored to its rightful owners."

"Or what?"

He was silent for several seconds, and she thought he might be having some kind of internal dialogue. "Or something very bad will happen."

"What?"

"I cannot tell you."

"Back to square one." She eyed the box. "What are you saying—that this thing is a bomb or something?"

"That is close enough."

A wave of cold swept over her. "Then why don't we just take it to the police?"

He tipped his head to the side, studying her. "Because the police will think I am as crazy as you do."

She swallowed. "That obvious, huh?"

"Yes. You assume I am…" There was another one of his pauses. "Schizophrenic."

"No," she answered when she was thinking she was in a car with a madman and a time bomb.

He gripped her arm. "Do not lie to me. Mental illness is your only reference. It is hard for you to believe that a spirit was trapped in the box. You think that is a…delusion."

When she didn't answer, he went on. "But you saw the mist shoot out of the box after Luke opened the final latch. The mist with the spirit of Zabastian. The warrior joined with Luke McMillan's mind and body. You know it, even if you do not want to admit it."

"Okay," she said because there was no use arguing. And in truth, she wasn't sure what to argue about. If Luke was delusional, then she wasn't going to change his mind. And if "Zabastian" was telling the truth, then she was in danger.

He began speaking again. "If we went to the police, we would have another problem, too. They will try to keep the box…as evidence. That will give the thieves the chance to acquire it again. So I must return the box to the Grand Master of the Moon. Only he can take advantage of its power."

Sidney turned and stared out the window, watching the wind blow a piece of crumpled paper down the sidewalk. She wanted to ask the man beside her to let her go. But where would that leave her and Luke?

As though he were following her thought process, he said, "You must stay with me, until we can turn the box over to its owners."

"Why?"

He kept his gaze fixed on her. "Because you are still in grave danger. If the men who attacked us cannot find the box and cannot find me, they will come after you." His voice was low and harsh. "They will torture you, and when you cannot give them the information, you will die painfully."

She winced. "That's pretty grim."

"It is the truth."

"Then what do you suggest we do?"

CARL PETERBALM HAD ENJOYED a very nice dinner at the Prime Rib, one of Baltimore's premier restaurants. Or, to put that in perspective, he had ordered a very nice dinner, starting with a double martini. He'd gulped the gin, but he hadn't done the rest of the meal justice because he'd been worrying about the shipment of antiques that he'd ordered from France.

He'd gotten it from a dealer who had promised him extra high value for his money. Neither one of them had mentioned the words "stolen goods," but that had been implicit in the transaction.

Either that or forgeries. It didn't matter which. You didn't get legitimate merchandise like this shipment for what he'd paid.

Carl had weighed the pros and cons and decided to accept the offer because he was determined to show his father that he could make a killing in the import business. Dad thought he was the only one who could make the big bucks, but Carl could do him one better.

So he'd ordered the merchandise and waited impatiently for it to arrive. The trouble was, once Sidney had started unwrapping the antiques, he'd gotten a very bad feeling.

It had something to do with that chest with the moon carvings. The moment he'd seen it, he'd felt a strange chill in the room, as if the box was haunted. And he'd thought Sidney felt it too.

Reluctant to start a discussion about it, he'd gone out to dinner to think about what he should do. He'd come to the conclusion that the box should be locked in the safe until he could get an opinion on it, so he started back to the office.

When he pulled into the garage, he saw that Sidney's car was still in its parking slot. He also noticed a strange smell in the air-like maybe some kids had been setting off fireworks. And he spotted some chips in the paint of some of the cement columns.

He'd have to speak to the management about making sure the place was secure, he thought as he hurried to the elevator.

Once he reached the third floor, he strode down the darkened hall toward the office where he'd left his research assistant.

She should be hard at work, but he didn't hear anything when he stepped into the outer office.

"Sidney?"

She didn't answer. Maybe she'd gone to the ladies' room or to the canteen to get something to eat.

As soon as he pushed into the room where she'd been working, he stopped short. The office was in shambles. The pitcher she'd unwrapped was lying in pieces on the floor.

The chair at the desk was overturned, and someone had pulled pieces of the shipment willy-nilly out of the cartons and thrown them around the room along with the packing materials.

In short, it looked like a hurricane had blown through the room. Well, not a hurricane—a person or persons, desperate to find something.

The box?

Now why was that the first thing he thought of?

Carl scrambled around the room looking for the antique. It appeared to be gone.

Why, and how?

Was Sidney working for someone sinister? Was this smashup a setup designed to make him think something bad had happened to her?

He reached for the phone to call the police. Before he could dial 911, he realized he couldn't get the law involved—not if the shipment was really stolen.

So now what? Maybe Sidney was somewhere hiding from whoever had done this?

If so, maybe he'd better get the hell out of here before they came looking for him.

He was about to leave when he heard a noise from the doorway. Spinning around, he got ready to duck behind the table.

"Mr. Peterbalm?" The question came from a woman who worked in one of the other offices. Betty something. He didn't remember her last name, but he'd seen Sidney talking to her.

"Yes," he breathed. "What happened here?"

She looked around, her eyes widening as she took in the mess.

"What happened?" he repeated.

"I don't know. I saw Sidney and Luke. They were running out of the office. They said there had been a robbery and I should hide."

"Luke McMillan?"

"Yes."

"What was he doing here?"

"A computer problem, I assume."

"There was a robbery? Did they call the cops?"

"They said not to." The woman looked around nervously. "Are you going to call the police now?"

"I'd better talk to the insurance company first," he improvised, hoping she'd buy the line.

"Oh right." She backed out of the room, and Carl followed, wondering what he was going to do now.

"WE HAVE TO FIND A place to hide out," Luke said, answering Sidney's question.

He was still trying to cope with his new reality. His thoughts were no longer private, his actions were no longer his own. And now his life was dedicated to saving a relic of the Moon Temple from robbers who would cheerfully kill him and Sidney if they could find them.

But if his thoughts were no longer private, neither were Zabastian's. The warrior was going to deliver the box back to its rightful owners if it killed him. And Luke along with him.

Luke's only advantage was that Zabastian had awakened in a totally strange environment. He knew nothing about twenty-first century America. And he was smart enough to realize that he needed Luke McMillan's help to survive here.

At the same time, a good portion of the warrior's thoughts were focused on Sidney. He wanted her, and he was going to seduce her, if he could manage it.

Luke wanted her, too. Had wanted her for a long time. And he hadn't been bold enough to do anything about it. A couple of minutes after waking up, Zabastian had pulled her on top of himself and started kissing her.

He laughed inwardly. If he were going to get shot by the Poisoned Ones, he might as well let Zabastian do his worst—or maybe it was his best—with Sidney.

Luke was still contemplating that scenario with happy anticipation when he caught another thought in the warrior's mind.

No, he inwardly screamed.

I have observed your world. I know what I'm doing, Zabastian's deep voice answered inside his head.

Luke felt his jaw muscles work. Words had come out of his mouth. It sounded like his voice. But he wasn't the one speaking. It was the warrior.

"Thank you for getting us out of the garage. I can drive now."

Sidney peered at him. "You're sure that's all right? I mean, aren't you having a…problem?"

Luke felt Zabastian give her his most charming smile. "It is my car. I know how to drive it."

"You're not talking like Luke."

He tipped his head to the side, looking at her, making silent assessments. Casually, he reached out and touched her shoulder. "It's me. He's just mixing up my speech patterns a little bit. Let me get behind the wheel. I know where we're going, so it makes more sense for me to drive."

She looked cautiously at him. Luke tried to make his fingers tighten on her shoulder, tried to warn her that the words coming out of his mouth were lies. But he wasn't the one calling the shots. Zabastian had taken over again. And this time he was going to get them into trouble.

He held his breath, waiting to see what Sidney would do. Unfortunately, she got out of the car and walked around to the passenger side.

Luke also climbed out and stood beside her on the darkened street. "You were fantastic," he said. He put his arms around her and pulled her against his body, stroking her hands over her back. "I never knew a woman who could handle herself with such bravery and style."

Despite his qualms about what the warrior had up his sleeve, Luke couldn't help admiring the smooth line.

Nor could he stop rejoicing in Sidney's reaction. A few minutes ago, she'd been questioning his sanity. It seemed, however, that she was still willing to respond to him.

Smoothly, Zabastian lowered his head to Sidney's. He stroked his lips over hers, sending tingles of heat shooting through Luke's blood. When his lips settled on hers, heat pooled in the lower part of his body.

He was instantly aroused. Instantly ready for sex.

In some part of his mind, he knew there was nothing they could do about it now, out here on the street. But he couldn't stop himself from going a little farther. Or, rather, stop Zabastian, since he was still the one in charge of this scene.

He went along for the very exciting ride, taking

greedy sips from her mouth as his hands stroked over her shoulders and back, then found her spine, playing his fingers up and down the delicate column.

Nice move, Luke thought as he heard her make a small sound of appreciation, felt her move against him, her middle pressing tantalizingly against his erection, telling him she craved the contact as much as he did.

With a practiced motion, his other hand traveled to her ribs, sliding up and down, then settling against the side of her breast, exploring the wonderful fullness of her.

She moved her head, languidly, invitingly. He found her tongue with his, delicately stroking, judging her reaction with satisfaction.

He might not be the greatest lover of the twenty-first century, but he knew when a woman was signaling that she wanted to go farther. Too bad the car was so small. There was no place to stretch out in the backseat. But maybe they could do it sitting up, with her in his lap.

Luke would have edged them toward the car, but Zabastian lifted his head.

"Not here," he said in a gritty voice. "We shouldn't stay out on the street."

Sidney blinked, and he saw her take in their surroundings.

"Let's get out of here." He helped her into the car, then walked around to the driver's door.

Luke hoped against hope that once he'd slid behind the wheel, Zabastian would turn the car over to him. But the warrior stayed in the driver's seat, literally and figuratively.

Luke tried to wrest away control. He might as well have tried to grab a piece of wood from the heart of a tree trunk.

Alarm flashed through him. *What the hell do you think you're doing?*

The warrior didn't bother to answer him. Instead he reached into Luke's mind and pulled out the information that he needed to drive the car.

Part of the information, anyway. He started the engine but didn't buckle up first.

Seat belt! Luke shouted.

Zabastian's eyes narrowed, but he took the time to access that bit of knowledge, then reached for the belt and pulled it across his chest, before fumbling the buckle into place. He also turned on the headlights.

Then he slammed the gear shift into reverse and started to back out of the parking space. Unfortunately, another car was coming up the street. As Zabastian tried to pull out in front of him, the other driver leaned on the horn, causing Zabastian to stomp on the brake, making the car rock from front to back.

"You okay?" Sidney asked, turning toward him.

"I'm just a little jumpy."

This time he looked up and down the narrow street and waited for another set of headlights to pass before propelling the car into the traffic lane.

But it was hardly a smooth exit. And when the warrior jammed the car into first gear, the vehicle lurched forward. Realizing the car was going too fast, he braked again.

It's not as easy as you think. There's a lot you have to do at once. That's why you need to pass a driving test before they let you loose with one of these machines.

Quiet! Let me concentrate.

Luke clamped his lips together as the car shot down

the street, almost sideswiping a couple of parked cars on the passenger side.

Sidney's gaze shot to him, and her eyes widened. "You're Zabastian!" she breathed.

Finally she'd figured it out. For all the good it did her.

His answer was immediate—and frighteningly arrogant. "I can do this."

Her body had gone rigid, and he heard her gasp as a set of headlights cut toward them on the narrow street. Luke wanted to close his eyes as the two cars practically locked chrome while they passed within inches of each other.

But closing his eyes wasn't going to make the nightmare go away. This wasn't a dream. He really was trapped inside his own body, forced to take a figurative backseat while a man who knew nothing about the twenty-first century tried to control a powerful sports car.

It's not like driving an oxen-drawn wagon, he inwardly muttered.

Apparently that was exactly the wrong thing to say. He'd dared to ridicule the warrior, and Zabastian was too proud to back down.

Instead of turning over the car to Luke, the warrior kept driving down the street, picking up speed as he went.

The streets of the inner city residential neighborhood were lined with typical Baltimore row houses interspersed with the restaurants and small markets and coffee shops that were the hallmark of the Greek neighborhood. It was still early in the evening, and the sidewalks were crowded with pedestrians.

A couple of people started to step into the crosswalk, then jumped back as the Beemer barreled toward them like a maddened rhino.

Beside him, Sidney held tight to the edge of her seat, her knuckles bloodless. She looked like she wanted to jump out of the car, but they were going too fast for that.

The vehicle turned the corner, then headed for the warehouse district near Fells Point.

Luke breathed out a sigh. At least they wouldn't be mowing down any people on the street here.

With the residential area behind them, Zabastian increased their speed.

"Stop," Sidney shouted. "You're going too fast. Let Luke take control of the car."

Luke felt determination harden his features, but he could not stop Zabastian.

Turning back to the road, he kept his hands on the wheel, his foot on the accelerator and his eyes straight ahead.

The car sped toward a cross street, right through a stop sign. Luckily there was nothing coming from the other direction, and they cleared the intersection without incident.

But their luck didn't hold. At the next intersection was a stoplight, and it was red.

Coming from the perpendicular street was a set of large, wide headlights moving rapidly toward them through the darkness

A truck. And it had the right of way.

"Stop!" Sidney shouted.

Luke added his silent admonition as he watched the vehicle speeding along the cross street, the driver obviously assuming that the car coming toward him was going to obey the traffic light and stop.

In this case, that was a fatal assumption.

From the corner of his eye he saw Sidney's face contort as she stared in shock at the huge vehicle that was now directly in their path.

Above the roaring in his ears, he could hear Sidney's voice shouting at the warrior.

"Stop. You're going to get us killed!"

Chapter Four

Luke could feel the confusion and the sudden panic welling up inside the warrior as he realized he was in over his head. The man had probably never asked for help in his life. But he needed it now.

"Give me control," Luke shouted, praying that the big Z wasn't too proud to prevent his own suicide—and their deaths along with his.

The cab of the truck had already entered the intersection. It was too dark to see the driver's face, but Luke could imagine the terror in the man's eyes as he realized the other driver wasn't going to stop.

At the last second, something inside Luke's mind snapped, and he regained control of his muscles. He wanted to slam down on the brake. Instead he eased his foot down, pumping the pedal and slowing the car as he yanked the wheel to the left to prevent a collision.

Somehow, he bought them enough time for the truck to roar past, the wind shaking the BMW.

Luke breathed out a sigh, giving Sidney a quick glance. When he turned back to the road, he got an unexpected shock. The left lane was blocked by a row of concrete barriers, and he was heading straight toward them.

It was impossible to avoid a collision. But at least they weren't going very fast when they slammed into the leading edge of the low wall.

The sound of crunching metal filled his ears as they came to a rocking stop.

You did that! the warrior shouted inside his head.

Shut up. There was no way to prevent it.

Had the truck driver seen the crash? Probably, but he apparently didn't want to get mixed up with the maniac who was driving the Beemer. The ruined Beemer. The car he'd lovingly restored.

Sidney was sitting in the passenger seat, staring through the windshield, looking dazed.

"Are you okay?" he asked urgently.

"I flew forward," she whispered. "But the seatbelt pulled me back. Otherwise, my head would have smashed into the glass."

With hands that weren't quite steady, he unhooked his seatbelt and staggered out of the car. He wanted to inspect the crumpled front end of his Beemer, but there was nothing he could do about it now. And he wasn't going to agonize over the car when Sidney might need him. He went around to the passenger side, where Sidney was still staring out the windshield.

"Are you all right?" he asked again.

She gave a small nod.

"Answer me."

"I…I'm okay."

He helped her out of the car, then gathered her close. Despite the circumstances, he liked the way her body melted against his and the way her arms came up to clasp him.

They stood swaying on the sidewalk, and he lowered his head, skimming his lips against her hair, her ear. He moved his hands up and down her arms, feeling her sway like a young tree in a wind storm. "Your legs are okay? Your neck?"

He felt her testing various muscles. "I'm okay. You have a good headrest."

"Does anything hurt?"

"I don't think so."

He nodded, then muttered, "I'm sorry."

She raised her face to his, her eyes questioning. "For what?"

"For bashing into that barrier."

She looked around. "Nobody expects a barrier in the left lane."

"Yeah." He'd wanted to get closer to Sidney for so long, and here they were, holding each other again for the third time in a few hours. This crazy situation was pulling them together. In order to reap the benefits, he had to keep them alive.

A voice inside his head—the voice that kept butting in—interrupted his thoughts.

Get the box!

The box. He cursed under his breath. He'd like to pitch the box into the Inner Harbor. But apparently Zabastian was right there doing his job.

Reluctantly, Luke let go of Sidney, then reached inside the car and retrieved the antique.

His mind was starting to focus on business again. Zabastian's business. Had the driver of the truck called the cops? And were the Poisoned Ones monitoring police communications?

He looked at the front of the car again. It was going to be a while before he got his prized possession back in driving shape—if he ever got the chance.

As he stood beside Sidney on the sidewalk, he heard a siren in the distance.

"We must leave," he heard himself say, even when he'd like to surrender to the cops.

That is not an option.

I was just indulging in a tempting fantasy.

He grabbed Sidney's hand. "Come on."

She seemed to emerge from a fog, looking around for an escape route.

"Where?"

They were hemmed in by a chain link fence that closed off the parking lot of a warehouse to their right. And if they crossed the street, they'd be right in the head-lights of any oncoming police cars.

As the sirens drew closer, Luke pointed up the narrow sidewalk. "This way."

Quickly he led her along the fence, hurrying to round the corner before the cops arrived.

He knew she was struggling to keep up with his long-legged strides. And he could hear her breathing hard as they reached the end of the block, then put the side of the building between themselves and the car.

"I have a stitch in my side," she gasped. "Can we rest?"

"Not yet."

Ahead of them he could see that the neighborhood changed again, back to an older residential area lined with row houses.

He kept pounding up the street, then through a pas-sageway between two houses.

At the other end of the passageway, Sidney stopped and leaned against the wall.

He gave her a couple of minutes before murmuring, "We'd better go."

They hurried through the backyard of a row house, then into the alley. A few more houses down the block, a man was standing outside, smoking a cigarette.

"Don't look at him. We don't want him to remember us if anyone asks. Walk normally, like we're just a man and a woman out for an evening stroll."

To reinforce the impression, he reached down and clasped her hand, then knit his fingers with hers.

They continued up the alley, holding hands. Did they look normal? He hoped so. At the same time, he hoped he could do a better job of sorting out his thought processes. Having the warrior in his head was a constant strain.

"The Poisoned Ones may show up at the accident scene," he said, surprised and a little alarmed that he'd used Zabastian's terminology.

He didn't like the implications, but he had more immediate issues to deal with. He and Sidney were on foot, and that put them at a disadvantage, since he knew the bad guys had at least one car.

Would the Poisoned Ones keep looking for them close to Peterbalm's office, or would they spread out over the city?

As they walked, Luke scanned the working class neighborhood that bordered the warehouse district. Each house had its own rectangular backyard, most marked off by chain link or high wooden fences. Sometimes there was a detached garage at the end of the yard. Sometimes a parking pad.

A lot of the cars were old and battered, which was a plus, as far as Luke was concerned.

Since high school, he'd done his best to forget about his checkered past when he and his friends had boosted more than a few cars and gone joyriding in them.

Lucky for him he'd never gotten caught, although he'd had some close calls.

Good, the warrior commented.

Good that I know how to steal a car? Or good that I didn't get caught?

Both.

I guess it was easier to steal an oxcart.

If you got caught, they chopped off your hand. Or your head—if you were unlucky.

He winced, switched away from the internal conversation and thought about the immediate problem. Being technically oriented, he still remembered the basic method of hot-wiring a car. Unfortunately, it only worked in older models.

As he thought about twisting wires together, he felt the big Z eavesdropping with extreme interest.

Thinking about a life of crime? Luke silently asked.

I'm trying to survive in your world.

A car will get us out of here. But criminals rarely escape the law for long.

He began walking more slowly, testing the door handles on the vehicles he passed. When he came to one that was unlocked, he stopped and looked around, grateful for the darkness.

He turned to Sidney. "I'm going to try and cross the wires on this wreck. If the cops come, start running." He walked to the gate of the nearest yard and made sure it opened. Then he looked inside and saw one of the passages that led between the houses.

Pointing, he said, "Go that way."

"What about you?"

"I'll catch up." He hesitated, then overruled Zabastian's objection and handed Sidney the box.

She stared at him in surprise. "What if we get separated?"

"I can find you."

"How?"

"There is something inside me that…" He hesitated, then finished, "That lets me home in on the box."

"You—meaning Zabastian—can do that?"

"Yeah."

She dragged in a breath. "Okay."

Probably she didn't believe him. Luke wasn't sure he believed it himself. But he felt the big Z's absolute conviction.

Unfortunately, the only way to prove it was to lose the damn thing. And he wasn't planning to do that if he could help it.

Don't even think about it, the warrior warned.

He opened the door of the car and immediately started coughing. It smelled like whoever owned this vehicle must be a chain smoker. The ashtray full of butts proved the point.

Luke pulled out the ashtray and pitched the contents into a patch of weeds. Then he returned to the car. Emptying the butts helped. But the air was still strong enough to cut with a knife.

What in the name of the full moon is that stuff?

Cigarettes.

Did someone poison the car?

Yeah, but the guy who drives it likes this particular brand of poison. It's from a product he smokes. If he's unlucky, it will kill him. If he's lucky, it will only shorten his life.

Luke cut off the interior conversation as he slid onto the dirty floor under the steering column and turned on the small flashlight attached to his key ring so he could peer at the tangle of wires.

He hadn't done this kind of job in years, and it took several minutes for him to get his bearings.

He sorted through electrical connections, then tried a combination of wires.

Nothing happened and he cursed under his breath.

You know how to do this?

Shut up.

SIDNEY WATCHED LUKE CROUCHING on the floor below the dashboard. He was going to hot-wire the car. And while he was busy, she had her own agenda.

She'd grabbed her cell phone on the way out of the office and slid it into the pocket of her pants, but she hadn't been able to call for help. Now she had the chance to do it.

Quietly she walked a couple of yards from the car and pulled out the phone.

Fingers crossed, she pressed the end button to activate the instrument. She knew the battery was low, and she was hoping there were still enough bars left to make a call.

When she got a dial tone, she sighed with relief.

Sabrina was on her speed dial, and she quickly worked

the control buttons. The phone rang once, twice, three times, and she held her breath, praying that her friend hadn't left for dinner yet.

She'd almost given up hope when the other woman answered.

"Sabrina! Thank God."

"Sidney?"

"Yes."

"What's wrong?"

Now that she had her friend on the line, she realized how strange her problem was going to sound. "I don't know where to start."

"Just go slow and tell me what's wrong."

She dragged in a breath and let it out in a rush. "That box. You said it belonged to a religious cult."

"Yes."

"Men came into the office and tried to steal it. They started shooting."

Sabrina made a strangled sound. "Are you shot? Are you okay?"

"They didn't hurt me."

"Thank God."

She glanced over at the car, seeing Luke's legs sticking out the driver's door. What would he do if he caught her on the phone? Well, not Luke. Zabastian. So was she saying she believed in the warrior? As nutty as it seemed, she knew she had bought into the explanation for Luke's odd behavior.

"I'm on the run," she told Sabrina.

"Where are you?"

"In an alley. I'm not sure where, exactly." She dragged in a breath and let it out. "This is going to sound crazy."

"Is the box stolen? Is that it?"

Sidney gasped. "What makes you think so?"

Sabrina hesitated a moment. "Your description. It's too valuable to come in a random antique shipment. Did the owners come after it?"

"No. It was someone else. But let me back up. My computer broke in the middle of the inventory, and Luke McMillan came to fix it. After he got it going again, he stuck around and started fiddling with the box and he opened it. And…and some mist came shooting out. Luke passed out, and when he woke up, he was somebody else. The spirit of an ancient warrior who's supposed to protect the box."

"What?"

"I knew you wouldn't believe me."

"I believe you!" Sabrina almost shouted into the phone. "Don't hang up. Enough strange things have happened to people at 43 Light Street that I believe things that would stop anybody else in their tracks. Just tell me what happened after that."

Sidney looked toward the car again. Luke was still busy. Hunching her shoulders, she turned away from him and walked a few feet farther down the alley. "We were in a car accident. We had to run away before the cops got there."

"Why?"

"Long story. I've got to talk fast, before he tries to stop me."

Sabrina's voice turned hard as ice. "He's kidnapped you?"

"Um…not Luke. The ancient warrior. When the men came to steal the box, we split. Luke says we have to get the box to the Master of the Moon. He says…"

Her sentence trailed off as a large hand lifted the phone out of her grasp.

"Sidney? Sidney?" Sabrina called from the other end of the line. But she was talking to herself now.

"What the hell do you think you are doing?" the man who held the phone asked, his voice deep and menacing. As he spoke, he clicked the off button.

She raised her chin. "Who are you—Luke or Zabastian?"

"Both. Answer my question. What were you doing?"

"Calling my friend Sabrina."

"Why?"

"We need help."

"I will be the judge of that."

"Like you were the judge of driving the car and wrecking it?"

He glared at her. "Get in the car. We have to get out of here."

When she didn't move, he took her firmly by the arm and marched her to the stolen vehicle.

She was about to climb into the passenger side when a door across the alley opened.

"Hey," a man's voice called in the dark. "What are you freaking doing with Eddie's car?"

A flashlight beam hit her in the face, and she raised her arm to shield her eyes.

The beam switched to Luke.

LUKE SWORE UNDER HIS breath. "I am a friend of Eddie," he answered. "He is lending the vehicle to me."

Stop talking like a robot, he shouted to the man inside his mind. But it was already too late.

"The hell you are. You sound weird. And I've never seen you around here before." As he spoke, the man stepped out of the door and walked rapidly down to the alley. "You'll get away from that car if you know what's good for you," he announced.

He was a large guy, over six feet tall and well built. Probably he had about fifty pounds on Luke, and he looked to be in his mid- to late twenties.

As he advanced, Luke glanced toward Sidney. "Get in the car," he shouted.

Instead, she took a step back. Was she going to run? He wanted to grab her, but he was too busy with Eddie's neighbor.

Zabastian let the guy get within striking distance, then reached out a hand and started to bring it down on the man's shoulder, near his neck.

No, Luke shouted inside his head. He knew that Zabastian intended a killing blow.

You can't kill him. We're stealing his neighbor's car. We're the ones in the wrong.

Somehow he stopped the blow in midair.

Zabastian bellowed, and Eddie's neighbor seized the opportunity to aim a right hook at Luke's jaw.

Luke ducked the blow, preparing to strike back. But Zabastian beat him to it. As the attacker charged forward again, Zabastian stiffened one finger and jabbed the man in the ribs. It didn't feel like a serious blow, but it must have hit a very sensitive spot for the man gave an anguished grunt and went down on his knees on the gravel parking pad.

"Come on." This time when Luke grabbed Sidney's arm, she let him help her into the car, then coughed when she took a breath of the smoke-stained air.

Luke ran around the other side and slid behind the wheel, setting the box on the seat between them.

She cleared her throat. "Let Luke do the driving."

"I am."

As he pulled out of the parking spot, he knew she was watching him carefully. Then she glanced back at the man on the ground.

"What did you do to him?"

"Not much. A maneuver I learned in my training."

"Your hands are deadly."

"Yes."

"Why didn't you kill the guys you call the Poisoned Ones?"

"I was getting used to Luke's body."

Sidney made a strangled sound, then gave him a direct look. "Where are we going?"

"I'm thinking." Luke was the one who answered, wracking his brain as he tried to come up with a hiding place.

SABRINA RAN DOWN THE hall to the front door and caught up with Dan just as he was about to step outside. They'd been on their way to dinner when the phone had rung. He'd told her to ignore it. She'd had a premonition that she should answer, so she'd gone back to the kitchen.

Dan studied the look on her face. "What's wrong?"

She clasped her hands in front of her, trying to keep them from shaking.

Seeing the reaction, Dan quickly crossed to her, holding her close. "You'd better tell me."

"I want to. But it's hard to explain. I mean, it sounds damn weird. Or it would if you weren't a member of the 43 Light Street group."

"Something nobody else would believe?" he asked, his deep voice and his strong arms comforting her.

She hitched in a breath and let it out. "Sidney Weston is in trouble. She works for that importer, Carl Peterbalm."

"The guy the Light Street Detective Agency is investigating?"

"Right."

"And you're sure she isn't involved?"

"She's not. She called me earlier while she was unwrapping a shipment of antiques. One of them was a box. She described it to me, and it sounded like an artifact from the Moon cult. She never would have done that if she was helping Peterbalm import stolen merchandise."

"Okay. But what's the Moon cult?"

"A religion from the ancient world. I was going to look at the box tomorrow because it could be the proof you need to nail Peterbalm. But gunmen broke into the office. It sounds like they would have gotten the box, but Sidney had called in a computer guy, Luke McMillan, because she was having problems. He got her out of there safely. Well, not just him."

She stepped far enough away so that she could meet Dan's eyes. "Before the gunmen arrived, some kind of mist floated out of the box and knocked Luke out. When he came to, he said he was an ancient warrior sent to protect the box."

"Oh brother."

She searched his face. "You think that's a delusion?"

"You talked to Sidney, and you believe it's true. That's good enough for me."

She felt some of the tightness in her chest ease. "Thank you."

"Like you said, some weird things have happened to the Light Street group." He thought for a moment. "You're saying that this warrior is sharing Luke's body?"

"Something like that."

They stared at each other.

"Like us," he said slowly.

She felt a chill skitter over her skin. "My Lord, I wasn't even thinking about that," she breathed. When she and Dan had met years ago, they'd discovered they were the reincarnations of lovers separated by death two hundred years earlier. "But they weren't controlling us," she said to Dan. "I get the feeling this warrior guy has some control over Luke's body."

Dan's eyes narrowed. "Think about what that must be like. That could drive you crazy."

She winced as she took in the full implications of Luke McMillan's predicament.

"I hope he's got the strength to deal with it."

"Yes," she answered, praying that Luke wouldn't fall apart—not while he and Sidney were in danger.

Dan kept his gaze on her. "Is there anything else I should know?"

She swallowed. "Unfortunately. I think they may be on the run from the police, too."

"Why?"

"They ran away from an accident scene." She focused on the details of the conversation with Sidney. "When he found out she was talking to me, he took the phone away from her. But before he turned it off, I could hear him in the background. And he didn't sound like a computer guy."

"He sounded like an ancient warrior?"

She considered the question. "Well, as much as a modern man could sound like that."

"So what are we going to do about it?"

"Sidney called me because she thinks they need help. But he doesn't." She turned one hand palm up. "We have to find them."

"Yeah. But if he's not cooperating, I don't think she's going to call you again. And what if we can find them? Is the warrior going to kill us before we can get it through his head that we're trying to help?"

Sabrina thought about that. "I guess we need a team of tough guys from the Light Street Detective Agency and Randolph Security."

LUKE DROVE DOWN THE alley, then turned right and onto one of the narrow streets. He took several turns, aware that Sidney was watching him.

"You don't know where you're going?" she accused.

"I'm looking for something," he muttered.

"What?"

"Different license plates for this car."

"Huh?"

"We're in a stolen vehicle, in case you don't remember that scene a little while ago. If that guy turns in a description of the car to the cops, I want different plates."

"More stealing?"

"Sorry."

He pulled to a stop beside another junker car and waited for several minutes, watching the houses on either side of the alley, trying to see if anyone was looking out the window or standing on a porch.

Finally, he reached for the handle, then turned back to Sidney.

"Can I trust you to stay in the car this time and warn me if you see anyone coming?"

"Yes."

He gave her a long look, then watched her slump down in her seat.

Mercifully, Zabastian had been silent for several minutes. But as Luke climbed out of the car, the warrior sent him a thought.

She's cooperating for the moment. But you must learn to control her better.

Annoyance shot through Luke. *I'm not the boss of her.*

A woman must listen when a man speaks.

Not in this world. In the twenty-first century, women are the equal of men.

You must be making a joke!

Stick around, and you'll find out.

Luke squatted beside the car, keeping one eye peeled for trouble and hoping he wasn't going to get shot when he started working on the license plates.

Chapter Five

To Luke's relief, he was able to remove the license plates in the dark and exchange them without incident. With thanks to God for small favors, he drove away from the scene of the new crime, his mind still scrambling to think of a place to hide out.

"Where are we going?" Sidney asked again.

As if by magic, an address leaped into his mind.

"We can go to the house of some friends. Ginny and Tom Hanover. They were some of my first customers. I've been fixing their computers for years."

"Won't we put them in danger?"

He shook his head. "I had dinner there a week ago, and they told me they were going to spend a month in Mexico."

"And they don't mind lending you their house?" Sidney pressed.

"I hope not." The answer came out more sharply than he intended, and he knew this situation was getting to him. His life was out of control, and every time he turned around, he got into a worse fix. He wished he'd never opened that damn box.

Then Sidney would be in bad trouble, Zabastian was kind enough to remind him.

"Yeah."

"What?" Sidney asked.

He sighed. "Just talking to myself again."

She tipped her head to the side, staring at him. "You mean, you're talking to the warrior? And you said it out loud."

She looked like she didn't expect him to be straight with her. But he answered with a simple, "Yes."

"And you and I…" She swallowed, then started again. "I'm talking to Luke McMillan now."

"Yes."

"So what's it like? Channeling?"

"It's not exactly channeling. I'm not communing with someone who's dead. His spirit was in the box."

"Can you explain that?"

He sighed. "I'm not equipped to explain it."

She reached out and carefully laid her hand over his. "Can he feel that?"

"Yes. He feels everything I feel."

"How do you know?"

"I can tell when he's reacting."

"And he's listening to this conversation."

"Of course."

"Is he critiquing our discussion inside your head?"

"He's been quiet for a while."

Before Luke could enjoy that state of affairs, he felt the warrior getting ready to assert himself.

And Sidney didn't help by asking, "What's he thinking now?"

Luke struggled to keep the warrior's pointed observation silent. But Zabastian forced the issue by muttering, "That you should learn your place."

She folded her arms across her chest and turned to face him. "That's what he's thinking?"

"I'm afraid so. But he's operating on assumptions he learned a thousand years ago when social conditions were quite different. If you remember your ancient history, women weren't exactly equal partners back then."

She glared at him. For several moments she kept her lips pressed together. Then she said, "Okay, Zabastian. You're here now. But you never explained how you ended up in that box."

Luke was as interested in the answer as Sidney. He kept his eyes focused straight ahead of him, and listened intently to the words he spoke. "I was being punished."

"For what?"

"The Master of the Moon is very strict about how his servants behave."

Luke knew the man hated to say more. But at the same time, he seemed compelled to admit his sins. Since Luke had been carrying this man's consciousness around inside himself for the past six hours, he felt the warrior's internal struggle.

The answer rose up from deep inside the man's psyche. "I killed a woman," he said.

Sidney gasped, and Luke felt his own jolt of shock. He'd been in the ancient warrior's mind, but only on the surface. From the first, he'd considered the guy a badass. He hadn't known how bad.

Sidney shifted her body so that she was leaning as far away from him as she could get in the car. "Care to explain that piece of information?" she said.

"She was a woman named Devona, a priestess in the Temple of the Moon. She was new to the sacred sisters, and she was impatient to acquire more power for herself. She saw that Alana was in line to be chief priestess, so she poisoned her."

Luke felt the warrior's pain reverberating inside himself. But that was only part of the equation. The sentiments he heard inside his head were from another, more violent time, an ancient age when the rules of life were different from today's. But whatever the rules had been, the warrior had violated the laws of his society.

Sidney was watching him, watching the play of emotions across his face. "You loved Alana?" she said, her voice not quite steady.

"Yes," the warrior said, his voice soft. "We were very close. She called me to her, and she died in my arms. She suffered for many days, and she had time to think about who had hurt her and how it happened." He dragged in a breath and let it out. "She remembered that Devona brought her a drink the night before she got sick."

"That's not much evidence."

"It was unusual. That was why Alana noted it. When she told me what Devona had done, I...went crazy." His voice grew hard. "I am a warrior. I am trained to act. I forced Devona to confess."

"So you think that a confession under torture is valid?"

He made a harsh sound.

"Maybe you were wrong," Sidney said.

"I was not wrong!"

"Then you killed her?"

"Yes. But I should have let the priests take care of her

punishment. They were angry that I had overstepped the bounds of my…commission."

Luke wasn't sure he could have asked any more of the warrior, but Sidney apparently still had questions.

"And they put your spirit into the box?" she asked. "For all that time?"

"I have been out of that box seven times over the years. Each time I have defended the sacred object."

"And then you went back into your prison?" Sidney whispered. She reached over and laid a hand on him again. Luke could feel her warm fingers on his forearm.

"Yes. I must go back until I have served out my sentence."

"How will you know?"

"The priests will decide."

"When you're in the box, are you sleeping or are you aware of time passing?"

"I feel each second dragging by." He sighed. "It is a heavy burden."

"That must be horrible."

"I committed a crime, and I must live with the consequences," he said, his tone stoic.

Sidney was looking at him with new eyes. "Was Alana your lover?" she asked.

"Making love with her was forbidden. She was a priestess and I was a warrior."

Sidney nodded. "I'm sorry that the two of you couldn't…find happiness together."

"We lived by the Way of the Moon."

Luke heard the pride in the man's voice. His own voice, he realized. He hadn't understood Zabastian very well. He still couldn't completely figure out the man who had invaded his body, but Sidney's questions had helped unlock some of his secrets.

"Both men and women serve the Way of the Moon?" Sidney asked.

"Now it is only men."

"Why?"

"Because the priests took over all the duties when the order went underground."

"Why?" she pressed.

He gave her a quick look, then focused on the road again. "Because women are more ruled by their emotions than men."

"That's not always a bad thing," she murmured, and Luke could sense her emotions rising now. She was silent for several moments, and Luke waited for her to make some cutting remark.

But perhaps she was more interested in getting information than in challenging the warrior. Or perhaps she was also understanding him better. "Have you told any of this to anyone else since you went into the box?" Sidney asked.

"No. Nobody else ever wanted to know."

"I'm sorry," Sidney murmured.

"Why?"

"It added to your loneliness."

Luke felt his stomach muscles clench, and Sidney nodded.

After speaking so frankly, Zabastian sank back into himself. Maybe he was sorry he had revealed so much about his past and his punishment.

Or maybe it was a relief to get it off his chest. He was silent as they drove up Charles Street, to the northern part of Baltimore where the houses were large and situated on wooded lots. He found the street and made sure nobody was following him as he turned into the driveway and steered the junk car around to the back of the property.

SABRINA PACED THE LENGTH of the living room of the Roland Park house where she and Dan Cassidy lived.

When she heard him put down the phone, she whirled, her gaze going to his face.

His grave expression had her crossing the room and clutching his arm. "What did you find out?"

"Well, you were right about the car accident. A car belonging to Luke McMillan crashed into a concrete barrier in the warehouse district near Greektown. Before that, they almost hit a truck. The driver's voice was shaking when he called the cops."

"And Luke and Sidney were gone by the time the police arrived?"

"Yes."

As she tried to imagine what had happened to make them leave the scene of an accident, Dan asked, "Could Luke have been drunk? On drugs?"

"I don't know." She swallowed hard. "But maybe… you know…maybe the, uh, warrior could have been driving."

Dan made a frustrated gesture with his hand. "I don't know. I don't know Luke. And I don't know if what he told Sidney is even true. I mean, he could be mentally unstable. Or he could be fencing stolen merchandise for Carl Peterbalm."

Sabrina winced. "No."

"How well did Sidney know him?"

"She'd talked about him before. I know she liked him."

Dan made a rough sound. "He could be a charming sociopath."

"She told me how hard he worked at his computer business. And she made it sound like he was shy with her. That doesn't sound like a sociopath to me."

"How did he happen to show up at her office tonight?"

"I told you, the computer broke, and he came to fix it. Are you cross-examining me?"

"I'm trying to get the facts straight."

Sabrina clasped her hands in front of her. She loved Dan, but when he started interrogating her, she could understand why people made lawyer jokes. "Are the police looking for them?"

"Well, they're on the radar. But the cops have a lot of other stuff to worry about. So a one-car accident isn't going to be near the top of their list."

"Is that good or bad?"

He sighed. "I wish I knew."

She read the strained expression on his face. "What else?"

"Hunter, Nick and Jed went over to the Peterbalm offices," he said, referring to three of the men who worked for Randolph Security, which was tightly allied with the Light Street Detective Agency. "They found the office in a shambles. And in the garage they found shell casings and places where bullets plowed into the cement columns."

Sabrina's face contorted. "So that part's accurate."

Dan nodded.

"Can you start a search for Sidney and Luke in the area where the car was wrecked?"

"We're already on it."

"And what about the armed men who broke into the office?"

"We're looking for them, too." He shifted his weight from one foot to the other. "Jed downloaded a copy of the surveillance tapes from the building's security cameras."

"How did he do that?"

"Randolph Security proprietary information."

She made a sound that was almost a laugh. "In other words, you did it illegally."

"Yeah. But we didn't harm the originals. They're still in the cameras. So if their building security company wants to look at them, they're free to do it."

"Have you called the company?"

"That's not our job."

"So you know what the men look like?"

"Yes."

Another thought struck her, and she gave her husband a direct look. "Did you see the action in the garage?"

"Some of it. The camera wasn't at a great angle. But for what it's worth, it looks like Luke McMillan was trying to protect Sidney. He was under fire when he got the garage door open."

Sabrina winced. "Why didn't you tell me that in the first place?"

"I wanted to hear what Sidney said about him first." He looked at his watch. "I'm going down to Light Street to look at the tapes."

"And I'm coming with you."

"Yeah, I thought you'd say that."

SIDNEY WATCHED LUKE LOOK around. No doubt he was evaluating the property from a whole new point of view—as a hideout.

Lucky for them, the driveway was screened by a row of pine trees, and the backyard was planted with numerous bushes and trees so that you could barely see the houses on either side. Which was good, since the car they'd come in hardly looked like it belonged in this neighborhood.

"Come on."

After snatching up the chest, Luke got out of the car and she followed, taking a breath of the fresh air.

"So far, so good," Luke murmured.

Sidney nodded as she stared at the old Victorian house with a turret at the front and a wide-screened porch in back.

"The Hanovers are doing pretty well," she said.

"Tom is a good salesman. He moves a lot of medical equipment."

"Um."

They walked across the patio, through a door and into the screened porch. Before they reached the back door, Luke stopped beside a table with a group of flowerpots. He moved one holding pink and magenta impatiens and retrieved the house key.

"That's a dumb place to put it," Sidney said, then wished she had just kept her mouth shut. She was nervous, about being alone with Luke and with the warrior.

"Yeah, I've told them something similar. Not quite in those words. They did it anyway," he said over his shoulder as he opened the back door and ushered her into a huge kitchen with an island and granite countertops.

She saw Luke looking around and knew that Zabas-

tian was taking in the setup. At least, it didn't make sense
that it would be Luke. He'd been here before.

"They prepare food here?" the warrior asked.

"Yes."

"We should eat."

"I guess you're hungry after a few hundred years in
the box." As soon as the words were out of her mouth,
she decided it was another dumb thing to have said.
From now on, she vowed to think before she spoke.

"Do you think the Hanovers will mind us raiding their
pantry?" she asked.

"We can restock for them later."

"Restock? How long do you expect to be here?"

He shrugged. "It depends."

Feeling like she was trespassing, she pulled open the
refrigerator and looked to see what the owners had left.
There wasn't much, but she found some grapes in the
vegetable keeper and some Vermont cheddar cheese that
the homeowners hadn't cleared out before they left. Not
much of a meal, but it would have to do.

BECAUSE HE WAS NERVOUS about being here alone with
Sidney, Luke poked around in the kitchen. Opening the
freezer compartment, he pointed to some plastic cartons
that were carefully labeled.

"Ginny makes fantastic beef stew. We can thaw this
in the microwave, then heat it up."

"You're sure this is okay? I mean making ourselves
at home."

"They trust me."

"So when you tell them you were hiding out from
armed men, they'll understand?"

Nerves made his voice gruff. "Stop coming up with objections. We need to hole up here while we figure out where to find the Temple of the Moon."

"You don't think the phone directory will do?"

"No," he snapped, then turned away. Inside his mind, he knew the warrior wanted to tell the argumentative woman to shut up and fix a meal. But Luke knew that wasn't the way to handle her.

Handle? That wasn't the kind of relationship he wanted with Sidney. He wanted something real. Something that would endure.

Or was he kidding himself?

Unable to deal with her sarcasm or the tight feeling in his own chest, he turned away from her and wandered into the dining room, then the living room and the den.

Are these people rich? Zabastian asked after Luke had explained the large, flat TV screen.

No.

But this house is big. How many people live here?

Two.

I think twenty people could live here comfortably.

Not by current American standards.

You waste resources.

Probably.

He stopped beside the fireplace.

You keep this house warm with fire?

It's just for...ambiance.

The warrior snorted and picked up a cut glass pitcher sitting on one of the side shelves. *And the rooms are filled with valuable items.* Zabastian hefted the pitcher in his hand, then replaced it on the shelf.

They inherited some antiques from Ginny's mother.
They have many things here that they do not need.
They don't need your critique.

The aroma of well-seasoned stew reached him, and he turned back to the kitchen where Sidney was spooning the food into bowls. Apparently she'd automatically taken the woman's role, and he wished he'd thought to heat the food himself.

Why? the warrior asked.

Because I don't want her doing all the domestic work.
Women are made for that. And for making love.

Like I said, we treat them as equal partners now.
They're bankers, senators, doctors, lawyers.

Zabastian made a rough sound.

"What?" Sidney asked.

"Nothing. I was having a little exchange with my inner warrior."

"About what?"

"Modern mores."

She gave him a considering look. "He's still commenting on sex roles?"

"Yeah."

She sighed. "What do you want to drink?"

"Cold water. I can get it."

As he went to the cabinet he asked, "Can I get you some?"

"Thanks."

He took down two glasses and added ice cubes from the dispenser on the side of the refrigerator. Then he added cold water from the faucet.

Zabastian swirled the ice cubes in the glass, then took a sip of the water. *This is very cold, like from a high mountain stream. But it should be pure. Why does it have a funny taste?*

From the chemicals they put in at the water treatment plant.

He set down Sidney's glass, then pulled out a chair and joined her at the table.

The stew was hot from the microwave, and Luke blew on it. "You cooked it quickly," the warrior commented.

"It's already cooked. I just heated it."

Of course Luke knew that, but he wasn't going to stop the warrior from asking questions because he'd never been great at idle conversation. And the Big Z might as well fill the silence.

He took a small taste off the spoon, prepared for Ginny's excellent cooking, then felt the stunned expression on his face.

"What?" Sidney asked.

"This is…wonderful."

"Yes. It's good."

"You eat like this all the time?"

She tipped her head to the side, her gaze fixed on him. "It depends on how well the woman cooks."

He grunted.

"I guess the art of seasoning food has come a long way in the past couple thousand years," she added.

He bent to his bowl of stew, spooning up a chunk of meat and chewing enthusiastically.

Close your mouth when you eat, Luke inwardly muttered.

Why?

It's polite.

The warrior muttered something Luke couldn't understand, but he assumed it was a rude suggestion. Nevertheless, he complied, and when Luke glanced up, he and Sidney exchanged a long look. He wasn't sure exactly what it meant, but it warmed him.

She swallowed the food in her mouth. "So, Zabastian, when you defended the box before, did you take over another man's body?"

It was a very direct question, and it hung in the air between them.

Luke was as interested in the answer as Sidney. "Yes," the warrior said.

"And what happened after that?"

"After the crisis was over, I went back into the box."

"You didn't fight it?"

He felt his features harden. "The Master of the Moon is all-powerful."

"But according to you, the bad guys have gone after the box more than once."

"They want its power. They are persistent."

Luke sensed that the warrior might not be telling the whole truth. But it seemed that there was nothing he could do to force the issue.

So he went back to his stew. Actually, it was gratifying to experience the simple meal from Zabastian's point of view. It would have tasted ordinary to Luke, but now he could appreciate the expertly seasoned gravy, the tender meat and the chunks of vegetables in a new way.

Sidney finished first and ran water in her bowl in the sink. Then she started for the kitchen door.

"Where are you going?" he asked quickly.

"To look for the bathroom. If that's okay?"

"Fine."

"Where is it?"

"Across the living room and into the hallway. It's the door beyond the den."

He watched her hurry out of the room, and he felt mistrust welling up from within himself—mistrust emanating from the warrior.

She is up to something.

Unfortunately, I agree.

He quietly pushed back his chair and walked lightly across the living room, heading for the hallway where she'd disappeared.

She might be going to the bathroom, but she'd stopped in the den first.

The phone was in her hand, her shoulders were tense and she was quickly dialing a number.

He stepped up behind her, grabbed the phone and pushed his finger onto the button that clicked off the connection.

You need to learn how to handle your woman, the warrior muttered.

She's scared. She wants to talk to her friends.

Don't make excuses for her. Take her mind off her fear.

Chapter Six

Sidney's heart stopped—then started up again in double time. "What are you doing?"

"You first," the man who held her in his grasp growled. She stared into his glittering eyes. Was it Luke or Zabastian? Or both? She didn't know. She'd given up trying to figure out what to expect and from whom.

When she remained silent, he said, "I told you, it's safer if nobody knows where we are."

"But I don't think we can handle this on our own."

"I am the one with the experience. I will be the judge of that."

She knew who was speaking now, and she felt herself tremble in his arms. What was he going to do? Punish her? Kill her for disobedience, like he'd killed that other woman.

Instead he lowered his mouth to hers. She tried to speak, and his lips captured the sound. At the same time, she forgot what she had intended to say.

Had she wanted to stop him, or let him know she liked what he was doing?

She didn't know which. But whatever the comment

had been, it evaporated like mist as his lips moved over hers, hungry, insistent, arousing.

She made another sound, and this time she knew it rose from her own need.

She had liked Luke McMillan. Admired him. Wanted to explore what they might mean to each other.

She didn't know if she even liked the man who clasped her body against his, but he rocked her to her core.

Fear and need warred within her. Desire won. She knew she wanted him as she had never wanted anyone in her life.

The realization was shocking, an acknowledgment that she'd lost her good sense. Or was she helpless to resist the combination of the two men—the one she knew and the one she wanted to know?

Her knees would no longer support her, and she had to cling to his broad shoulders to stay on her feet.

When he lifted his head to stare down into her face, the emotions she saw overwhelmed her.

"Your eyes are so blue," he said, his voice gritty. "I have never seen eyes with that color before. They are beautiful. Like twin mountain lakes. I could drown in them."

Poetry? From the warrior or from Luke?

She hardly knew this man. Not nearly long enough for this. At the same time, she felt like she had known him for a thousand years.

He stared into her face for heartbeats, then set the box down on the floor before lowering his head toward hers again. This time she raised up on tiptoes, meeting him halfway.

The contact was like a bolt of hidden power, sizzling

along her nerve endings, swamping her senses. Heat from his large body seared her through the layers of their clothing.

Now that they were alone, now that they had the time to explore each other, she discovered very quickly that this man knew how to kiss—with his lips, his tongue, his teeth. He was masterful and sensual, overwhelming and subtle by turns.

She knew she was being kissed by a man who had devoted considerable time to studying the art. Had she been missing this all along with Luke McMillan? Or was this the other man, the one who had tried to dominate her?

He wasn't dominating now. He was giving and taking in equal measure, obviously pleased that she could play this game as well as he could.

She drank in the heady flavor of the man who held her so firmly in his arms, catching a primitive tang below the taste of the well-spiced meal they'd shared.

She clung to him while he angled his head, first one way and then the other, as though he were greedy to experience her every way he could and greedy to take the kiss to new levels of sensuality.

But it wasn't enough. Not for her. And apparently not for him, either. She felt one of his large hands slide down to her hips and work the hem of her blouse from the waistband of her slacks so that he could flatten his palm against her back and press her breasts against his chest.

His other hand slipped lower, cupping her bottom and pulling her against his erection.

She had never lost her head with a man, having always been cautious in her relationships. Maybe that was why she had never gotten together with Luke.

Now she was hot and needy, burning up from the inside out.

When she moved her hips against him, he made a sound of approval. She was lost in the male taste of him, the feel of his hard body, the sensuality of his hands moving over her.

The clothes they were wearing were in the way. Apparently he agreed, because he deftly unhooked the catch of her bra. With one part of her mind she thought it must be Luke doing it. No ancient warrior would know how to unfasten a bra.

He shifted her so he could push the cups out of the way as he swept her blouse up and lowered his head, pressing his cheek against one inner curve and then the other.

Her nipples had already contracted to tight points of sensation. When he sucked one into his mouth, she cried out with the intensity of it.

One hand found her other breast, squeezing her nipple between his thumb and finger, twisting and pulling, driving her to an unbearable level of need.

She reached between them, fumbling with the buttons of her blouse. Apparently he was too impatient for her to finish. With two hands, he grabbed the sides of the garment and pulled, tearing fabric and sending buttons bouncing around the room.

As she gasped in shock, he stepped back and tore at his shirt, ripping it off and tossing it onto the floor. He sent her blouse and bra after it, then pulled her close, sealing her body to his.

She gasped again at the feel of her naked breasts against his hair-roughened chest.

His hands grasped her shoulders, swaying her torso

against his, and she heard a rumble of approval in his throat.

She fumbled with the hook on her slacks, then finally lowered her zipper, pulling off her pants and panties as he held her in his arms. Then she tackled his jeans, tearing them off almost as quickly as she'd dispatched her own slacks.

He laughed softly. "Are you in a hurry?"

"Aren't you?"

"Yes," he answered.

Wrapping his arms around her, he took her down to the rug.

She closed her eyes so that she could focus on the physical sensation, expecting him to come down on top of her. But he rolled to his side, cradling her in his arms. While before he had been a whirlwind of motion, now he lay perfectly still, just holding her.

She felt the tension in him and also in herself.

She took a breath of the air. It was different than it had been only moments ago.

"I smell smoke," she whispered, alarm dancing through her.

"From the fire."

"Fire?" Her eyes blinked open, and she tried to figure out what she was seeing.

"To keep us warm."

She lifted her head and looked around. The room had been dark, except for the illumination from the hallway.

She remembered coming down the corridor to get here. But now the light seemed different. It had a strange, flickering quality. When she took a second look, she gasped.

As her eyes adjusted to the dim light, she saw that the modern surroundings had disappeared. Instead of a room in a Victorian house, they were somewhere else.

It couldn't be possible. But it was. They were in a cave and the red and gold, flickering light came from a wood fire, the smoke rising up and escaping through a hole in the roof.

Lifting her head, she stared at the stone walls that were painted with drawings of men and animals. Not the primitive cave paintings she associated with archeology expeditions, but quite sophisticated works of art.

Outside, the wind howled and ruffled the curtain of animal skin that blocked what she assumed was the entrance.

She moved her hand against the surface below them. It wasn't a rug anymore. Instead they were lying on animal skins, shaggy pelts from some beast she didn't recognize.

In a panic, she tried to push away from the man who held her in his arms, but his hands tightened on her shoulders.

"What have you done?" she demanded. "Where are we?"

"Another place."

"But how?"

"I am not sure. I wanted to be here with you, and it happened."

She tried to take that in. The explanation made no sense, but when had anything passed the sanity test since the mist had shot out of the box and Luke had fallen to the floor?

Raising her head, she stared at the man who lay beside her on the animal pelts. "Who are you?"

"The same man who was kissing you a few minutes ago."

"Luke?"

"Yes," he answered, but she wasn't sure she believed him.

"Are we going to get stuck here?" she asked.

"It would be a good place to hide."

"But are we stuck?" she pressed.

"No," he answered, but she had the feeling that he wasn't focused on their location. He was a man who wanted a woman, and he was determined to make it happen.

While the complexities of their situation spun in her mind, he cupped the back of her head and brought her mouth back to his.

A little while ago, their kiss had been frantic. This kiss was different. It was persuasive, almost sweet, as though he was trying to woo her and gentle her at the same time.

His lips moved over hers, his teeth gently nipping and teasing. Then his lips sipped from her, making her focus on the man, not the surroundings.

She didn't forget about the cave. But now it felt right for her to be here making love with him.

His hands stroked down her ribs, then teased the sides of her breasts, bringing her quickly back to the level of arousal where she had been a few minutes earlier.

When she moaned, he drank in the sound as his hands found the hard points of her nipples, teasing and inciting her.

"Luke," she whispered.

He made a grating sound deep in his throat, and she wondered if he was pleased with the name she had spoken.

She had known Luke McMillan for six months. She

had known Zabastian for seven hours. In that short time, she had found out he was bold, ruthless, reckless.

And a skillful lover.

She'd known men who took what they wanted from a woman and thought very little about their partner's needs.

This man had focused his total attention on her pleasure, and that couldn't help surprising her, especially after some of the things he'd said about women.

As he bent to suck one pebble-hard nipple into his mouth, his hands slid over her body, finding places she had never considered as erogenous zones. He rolled her to her back and circled her navel with the pad of his thumb in a way that made her blood simmer.

He knew the secrets of the human body, knew how to incite and soothe at the same time, keeping her balanced on a knife edge of arousal.

She wanted to beg him to slide his hand lower and dip into the aching place between her legs. But she knew it wouldn't do her any good. He was going to take his own time exploring the secrets of her body.

She was almost out of her mind with desire when he finally glided one hand into the wet heat of her sex, stroking her there, bringing her to a peak of need.

"Please," she begged.

He raised his head, looking down at her in the flickering light, his gaze burning into her.

Then he rose above her, his erection sliding against her throbbing body, raising her to another level of need.

She cried out when he entered her, stretching her and filling her.

His gaze was still on her face as he rolled her to her

side so that he could caress her with his hand while he moved in and out of her.

She heard his breathing turn harsh. Her own breath sawed in and out of her lungs as she clung to his shoulders, her hips moving in concert with his.

She sensed his need and also the discipline that came from deep within him.

She had never felt more connected to anyone, physically and emotionally.

As her pleasure built, she knew he was holding back waiting for her to reach the highest peak and tumble over before he allowed himself to follow her.

When his fingers stroked against her most sensitive flesh, she came undone as an orgasm exploded through her. He followed her into the white heat of pleasure, his shout of satisfaction echoing against the walls of the cave.

She collapsed against the primitive bed, struggling to catch her breath, stunned by the strength of her reaction to this man.

He stroked the damp hair back from her face, then cradled her sweat-slick body in his embrace.

What was he feeling now? She wanted to ask him where the two of them stood after that frantic coupling, yet she couldn't dredge up the words. She didn't want to hear that, for him, it had just been a meaningless joining, when it had been so much more for her.

And what would it prove if she asked and he answered? She knew from experience that men didn't necessarily tell women the truth. More than that, what could she expect from someone whose name she couldn't even be sure of?

Whom had she slept with? Luke *and* the warrior?

She shivered.

"What?"

Unable to ask any of the questions that churned in her mind, she whispered, "I'm cold."

"Of course. I'm sorry." He stroked a finger along her sweat-slick arm, then moved so that he could pull one of the pelts from underneath them and spread it over their naked bodies, fur side down, making a soft comforter against her skin.

In the warmth under the covering, she snuggled against him. His hand stroked over her forehead, making her drowsy, and she closed her eyes.

HE WATCHED SIDNEY SLEEP. As she nestled trustingly in his arms, he had a moment to catch his breath for the first time since the wild ride had begun.

The sex had been mind-blowing.

Is it always like that for you? Luke asked the man who had come blasting into his body.

No.

Luke considered the answer, then dug below the surface of the warrior's mind. *I guess it would be good after a three-hundred-year dry spell.*

He felt the warrior's throat—his own throat—tighten.

That is none of your business.

Um, you've made it my business.

It was weird to be having a silent argument with himself and feel his blood pressure climb.

He knew that the warrior was struggling to get control of his emotions. He was using some kind of yoga breathing or something, and Luke focused on the technique, which was quite effective.

When the warrior spoke again, his inner voice was calmer. *Few women have…the capacity to let themselves fully enjoy the pleasures of the body.*

Maybe where you come from. Here, women are as free as men to enjoy sex.

Women can never be as free. They must worry about getting pregnant.

We have ways to prevent it.

But you have diseases that people can catch by having sexual relations. Those diseases have always been with us.

I don't have one, Luke snapped. *And neither does she.*

You love her, the warrior said suddenly.

Don't be ridiculous. I don't know her that well.

You know her well enough to fall in love.

That's…crazy.

Is it?

Luke considered the statement. Was that why it had been so hard for him to approach Sidney—because he cared too much to be rejected?

I won her for you, the warrior said smugly.

Yeah. I guess your caveman tactics worked.

Inside his head, the other man chuckled. *Call it the direct approach.*

Luke contained his annoyance, then asked. *So where do the two of us go from here?*

We return the box to its rightful owners.

Easier said than done.

We must do it.

Or die trying? Luke asked.

Yes.

And I get to die along with you?

We will not fail.

Luke sighed inwardly. He'd come to Sidney's office to repair a computer and gotten a lot more than he bargained for.

You would defend her with your life, would you not? the warrior asked.

Yes.

The box is more important than the woman.

That depends on your point of view.

The box is more important than any one person or any relationship. Zabastian said that with a finality that sent a shiver over Luke's skin.

You believe me? the warrior asked.

I understand that's what you believe.

It was still strange to be holding the internal conversation, but Luke was coming to terms with the spirit of the man who was sharing his body. And Zabastian was making accommodations, too.

I am enjoying your body, the warrior said. *You keep your muscles and your heart in excellent working order. It is a good thing when a man honors his physical self.*

I try to keep in shape. Luke heaved in a breath. *You'll eventually leave me, right?*

Dead or alive.

Luke wanted to shout out a protest, but he knew it wasn't going to do him any good. More than that, he had taken too much of the warrior's personality inside himself, absorbed too many of his values to object.

And if he survived, he knew he would never be the same.

Will I remember you? Luke asked.

I do not know. I never stay around to find out.

The woman in his arms stirred. She would wake up soon. It was tempting to stroke her, to lull her to sleep and give her more time to rest.

Or more time for you to hold her?

And you.

I do not mind admitting that I like this. But we must stick to business.

You call making love business?

The warrior growled something deep in his throat, and Sidney stirred again.

SIDNEY DIDN'T KNOW HOW long she had slept. But when her eyes opened again, Luke was holding her in his arms, his gaze focused on the skin that closed the door of their incredible hideout.

"You didn't sleep?"

"It is better if I do not."

"Is it dangerous here?"

He looked toward the curtain that shielded the door of the cave. "This place is well hidden. But this is also a dangerous time."

She sat up, dragging the fur along with her so that her breasts were covered. "Dangerous how? Do we have men with guns chasing us down like the guys back in the twenty-first century?"

He climbed out of the bed and began picking up the clothing scattered around the floor. Apparently the items had followed them to the cave.

He was completely naked, and completely casual about walking around in front of her.

Accepting the opportunity he'd handed her, she took

a good look at him. In the flesh. Luke McMillan was as remarkable as in her fantasies.

But it was Zabastian who spoke to her. "Men in this time are armed with knives. With a knife, you have to get in closer to your enemy."

She winced.

"Back here they were after the box too?"

"Yes."

He handed her the apparel she'd discarded so hastily, and she put on her bra and shirt without getting out of the primitive bed. Until that moment, she'd forgotten that the buttons had scattered across the floor. Looking down to hide her blush, she pulled the front panels over the cups of her bra, then tied the tails of the shirt in a knot at her waist. That would have to do until she could borrow something from the people who lived in the house where Luke had taken her.

Her chest tightened as she glanced around the cave.

"What?"

Obviously, the internal twinge had been accompanied by a look of alarm.

"Can we get back where we belong?"

"Yes."

"How?"

"I'll lead you back."

"And if you got killed, would I be stuck here?" she blurted, then immediately regretted the question.

He looked thoughtful. "I do not know."

"Maybe we'd better leave." She grabbed her pants and stood up, turning her back as she pulled them on.

"You have a nice ass," he murmured. "But then, I knew that from stroking you."

She turned to face him, finding him shirtless, wearing only the jeans he'd worn to work. "You certainly know how to be subtle."

"I do not have time for subtle."

The clipped words made her focus on something that had been circling around in her mind. Something she wanted to know. Or did she?

She swallowed, then asked, "How did Luke end up at my office?"

"He came to fix the computer."

"Yes, but before that, when I held the box, I had an odd feeling…like it was connecting with my mind." She kept her eyes on him. "Did you find out about Luke from me? Did you arrange for the computer to break so he'd show up?"

He kept his gaze steady. "You think I could do that?"

She raised her chin. "When you were in the box, you'd have to have a way to know what was going on in the outside world. I think you were using me."

His face hardened. "All right. Yes, I did that."

She caught her breath. "Can you still read my mind?"

"No. That is only when I am in the box."

She answered with a tight nod.

He pulled on his shoes and tightened the laces.

"You tricked me. And Luke."

"I did what I had to do."

"That doesn't make me like you."

"But we're both richer from knowing each other," he said with deep conviction.

Honesty made her admit that was true. Still, she heard herself say, "I like a choice when it comes to men."

"Have your choices been good?"

"Not that good. Except for Luke."

He didn't answer, but his face softened. When he reached toward her, she hesitated for a fraction of a second, then let her clasp her hand in his. It was warm and strong and reassuring, but she still didn't entirely trust him. She wanted to continue the conversation, to find out where she stood with Luke and Zabastian, but he cut off the discussion.

"Come on. We can't stay here." He moved her quickly across the cave.

Frigid air was seeping in around the edge of the curtain, and she felt goose bumps pepper her skin. Not just from the cold.

When he pulled the flap aside with his free hand, she gasped as she took in the unfamiliar surroundings.

Spread before her was a scene that could have been filmed in the Colorado Rockies. Only this was no movie. It was real. And she was viewing it from the vantage point of a high ledge cut from the native rock.

She could see a valley far below her, with a river of very blue water. Jagged peaks and sheer rock faces surrounded the sheltered valley. Above her the sky was an impossibly crystal blue.

The air felt different, so did the light. And how had they gotten up so high without flying?

She had never seen this place before, but she was certain it was nowhere near Baltimore.

Underfoot, the rock was slick with ice, and the man beside her tightened his grip on her hand. For several heartbeats, the scene held steady. Then it wavered, and Sidney tried to catch her breath again. They were hundreds of feet in the air. If she lost her footing, she was a dead woman.

Chapter Seven

"Close your eyes," the man beside Sidney advised as he tightened his hold on her hand.

She clung to him with every shred of strength she possessed. She hated being frightened, but this was so beyond her experience that she had no reference point.

As they stood on the high plateau, she felt a change in the texture of the air. It was thicker and less pure. Then a car horn blasted somewhere nearby.

Her eyes blinked open and she saw they were back in the Hanovers' house.

"We're home!" she whispered. "Thank God."

He turned to look at her. "You thought we couldn't return to your own time?"

"I didn't know. I don't have any experience with…time travel." She turned her questioning gaze toward him. "Is that what you call it? How did we do that?"

"The Moon Priests lent me some of their…I guess you'd call it magic."

"Magic. Right. Is that how you got into my head?"

"We will not speak of that again," he clipped out, and she knew that discussion was finished. "We must focus on my primary mission—returning the box to the Moon Priests."

"How come I never heard of them before today?"

He turned his free hand palm up. "They don't go around advertising their presence."

"You're sure they still exist in my time? You're sure you haven't taken possession of a box you can't return?"

"Yes!"

"How do you know?"

"I feel the vibrations of their presence."

He said it very casually, and she looked down, then found her gaze traveling to his naked chest. He'd left his shirt back in the cave.

He saw her studying him and said, "I should get dressed."

"Your friends won't mind if you take clothes?"

"We're running a tab."

He led Sidney up the stairs, down the hall past a home office, and into one of the bedrooms where he began opening drawers. When he found a pile of T-shirts, he took a black one out, running his fingers over the soft fabric before putting it on.

"Maybe I should change shirts, too," she murmured, turning to the closet and taking out an apricot colored blouse. "You're sure it's okay to use this?"

"Yes. Ginny will understand, when I tell her we were being chased by psychotic killers."

She made a strangled sound, then stepped into the bathroom to take off her ruined shirt and drop it in the trash can before pulling on the blouse.

Through the door, Luke said, "You don't believe in…vibrations?"

She opened the door. "Not usually. That's new age stuff."

"New age! It is very old, actually." He regarded her thoughtfully. "The world is more than the things you can know through your five senses. It is a mistake not to include the invisible world in your calculations."

She kept her gaze on him, assessing, marveling. "This is a conversation I never would have expected to have with Luke. Where is he?"

"I'm here." After a pause, he added, "We're getting more integrated." The phrasing and the voice sounded more like the man she knew, and she realized the comment had really come from Luke.

She studied his face. The features were the same, but now there was a subtle difference in his visage. This person's face was harder, more determined. More savage.

"Is that good?" she asked. "Integration?"

"It's less confusing for me."

"Not to me."

"Think of us as one person."

"Okay, but is Zabastian in control?" she asked.

He sighed. "Sometimes."

She nodded. "How do you know the Moon Cult is here—aside from vibrations?"

He shot her an annoyed look. "Not just vibrations. I know because your world is still here. But it is in grave danger."

CARL PETERBALM HAD DECIDED on the direct approach. He pulled into the parking lot in front of Sidney's building and looked around. Her apartment was in the far corner of a low-rise garden complex in Baltimore County. He'd never been here before, but he'd looked up her address in the company records.

He wanted to know what was going on, but he didn't want to speak to her over the phone and leave a record.

He got out and looked around, taking in details. In the illumination from several overhead lights, he saw that Sidney's building wasn't exactly the garden spot of the county. It bordered a patch of scraggly woods dotted with trash, the lawn was crisscrossed by footpaths and all around he saw neglect.

Couldn't she afford anything better?

He barked out a laugh. Well, maybe not on what he was paying her. So had she gotten mixed up with the mob or something? Had they come after her for a gambling debt and trashed his office?

He checked the address once more, wishing he could turn around and leave. This place gave him the creeps. But he needed to find Sidney, so he scanned the mail-boxes and found her name, then went to apartment 3A, on the ground floor.

Not a very secure location, he thought as he pounded on the door and waited. Then pounded again. No answer.

He called out her name, but she was still silent.

When he pounded again, the door across the hall opened and a large man stepped out. He was wearing sweatpants and a T-shirt that barely covered his bulging belly.

"Cut the racket," he said.

"Have you see Sidney Weston?"

"Naw. She usually comes home around six, but I ain't seen her."

The man eyed Carl for a few more seconds, then ducked back into his apartment and slammed the door.

Carl might have kicked Sidney's door, except that he didn't want to tangle with the neighbor again. So he turned to leave.

As he started toward the entrance, he heard a car door slam and looked up. In the light from the streetlamp, he saw three short, dark-skinned men standing on the sidewalk. As if they were all controlled by the same game box, they turned and marched up the walk to the apartment building. They might be wearing business suits, but they looked more like mob enforcers or hired assassins. And they were heading for the same building that he'd entered.

Were they the guys who had wrecked the office? They certainly looked capable of violence.

Maybe they hadn't seen him, since he was in shadow in the stairwell, and they were under the streetlight.

He scrambled frantically for an escape plan, but, unfamiliar with the complex layout, came up with nothing.

He debated just walking past them like he was a resident of the building. But his hands were shaking so badly that he knew he'd look guilty of something.

Quickly he turned and headed down the stairs, praying he'd make it to his car alive.

SIDNEY FELT AN ICY CHILL skitter over her skin. "What kind of danger is my world in? You told me before that the box could be like a bomb. Do you mean something else, like a terrorist attack? Do you have some inside information?"

"Your world—isn't it in chaos? Wars, diseases and the terrorists you spoke of?"

"Yes," she murmured.

"It is the honor and the privilege of the Moon Priests to watch over the world of men."

Sidney tipped her head to the side. "Then why are we in such bad shape?"

"Because they have lost some of their power and they can no longer guard you effectively."

"Wait a minute. Are you telling me that they lost the box a long time ago?"

"Yes," he answered, the syllable coming out hard and clipped.

"But you're supposed to be protecting it. Why didn't you come out of it and bring it back like you're doing now?"

"Because there was no one suitable to help me. My body wasn't in the box. Just my spirit. And I cannot simply possess the air. I must have a man who is strong enough to take my essence without dying."

She gasped as she caught the magnitude of that last statement.

"You dragged Luke to my office, knowing you could have killed him when you shot out of that box? Thanks a lot!"

"It was a calculated risk. And when he arrived, I was very confident in him. If he did not have a strong mind, he would never have worked the puzzle."

"Oh great," Luke muttered. The two of them might be "integrated" but he was still capable of joining the conversation on his own, if his feelings were strong enough. "Thanks for telling me."

"You are a good partner," Zabastian said, and Sidney knew he was still talking to Luke.

He fell silent and she stared at him. She had the feeling the two men inside Luke's body were still talking to each other, only now the exchange was completely silent.

Zabastian finally turned to her and gave her a sharp look. "You tried to call your friend. Can I trust you not to make any more calls?"

His voice was none too gentle. Not like the way Luke had always treated her.

But everything had changed this evening.

She licked her lips. Not long ago, this man had been her lover—one of the most skilled and considerate lovers she had ever had. But she still didn't know if something real had happened between them, or whether she could trust *him*.

She heaved in a sigh and let it out. At least she knew he wanted her to stay with him, and that meant he was prepared to protect her.

Was the Light Street group a better bet? She didn't know. And she had the feeling she wasn't going to get the chance to find out.

WITH HIS HEART BLOCKING his windpipe, Carl dashed through the door and into a hallway. He ran past a laundry room till at the end of the hall he found a door to the outside of the building.

With a sigh of relief, he rushed out into the night, then stopped to drag in huge drafts of air. When he no longer looked and felt like demons were after him, he started for the side of the building, then slipped into the woods, brambles tearing at his pants legs as he worked his way around toward his car. He had almost reached the front of the building when the sound of breaking glass made him stop in his tracks. While he'd been in the basement, the men had come around the side of Sidney's apartment. They were on a patio, where one of them had heaved a paving stone through the sliding glass door.

It was safety glass, and once they'd broken through, rounded chips began falling out of the hole and dropping to the ground.

Carl watched from behind a tree trunk large enough to conceal his girth. He tried to slip away before they saw him, but his legs simply wouldn't work. Instead he stayed where he was, gripping the tree bark to keep from slipping to the ground.

One of the men must have been wearing gloves because he reached toward the window and began enlarging the hole in the safety glass. When it was passable, the three men slipped into the apartment and disappeared.

Carl breathed out a sigh. Whatever was happening with Sidney was getting out of control.

This couldn't be about the shipment of antiques… could it?

A stray thought struck him, and he cringed. What if some of the antiques belonged to *them* and they were just trying to get their property back?

He cursed under his breath. He'd hate for these guys to be in the right. And even if they were, they were dangerous. He should call the cops, but he didn't want them to trace the call back to his cell phone. Nor did he want to seem like he was involved.

Teeth clenched, he pushed away from the tree, swaying on his legs for a moment. When he thought he could move, he ran as fast as he could through the woods and emerged on the sidewalk.

He made a strangled sound when he saw the nosy neighbor standing in front of his car, taking down his license number.

Lord, no!

Without thinking about what he was doing, he leaped forward, knocking the piece of paper and pencil out of the man's hand.

"Hey!"

The man gave Carl a murderous look and lunged. "You!"

Carl had never been particularly quick on his feet, but under duress he was able to dance back, avoiding a blow. "You don't want me! You want the guys who are robbing her apartment," he shouted.

"What?"

"They broke the sliding glass door. They're in there. Call the cops."

The man blinked. "Huh?"

Carl snatched up the paper with the license number, praying that the guy wasn't smart enough to remember a string of letters and numbers. Damn, he should have smeared mud on the plate. But it was too late for that now.

He was in over his head. And he didn't know what the hell to do besides get out of there.

The nosy neighbor started back toward the apartment. Was the poor jerk walking into a death trap? Carl didn't know. But at the moment the important thing was saving his own bacon.

He jumped in his car and backed out of the space, just as the three men came around the side of the apartment, their expressions angry.

Carl hit the accelerator and sped out of the parking lot, praying for the first time in his life.

LUKE WANTED TO SCREAM AT the bastard inside his head to leave him the hell alone. He could see Sidney was wondering whether to trust him, and he wanted to take her in his arms and use some gentle persuasion.

He'd finally connected with her, and despite the smug warrior's assumptions, making love with her had had as much to do with Luke McMillan as Zabastian. He knew how to satisfy a woman, even if he didn't know some of the warrior's fancy moves.

Okay, you had as much to do with it as I did.

Shut up.

I'm acknowledging your contribution.

Shut up.

I will. We can have this discussion later. We have to find the Master of the Moon.

And how are we going to do it?

I need your help.

Luke sighed. *Oh yeah? What kind of help?*

As soon as I understood something of the computer, I knew you would be an asset.

Luke looked back at Sidney. *Okay. I'll do a Web search, if that's what you want. But let me talk to Sidney first. She's got to be wondering why I'm blowing hot and cold with her.*

You can manage your love life later.

Not just my love life. You're pretty wound up with her.

But she cannot be my greatest concern. I am pledged to defend the box.

The box. Yeah.

Luke sighed. He was stuck. And the faster he did what the Big Z wanted, the faster he was going to square things with Sidney.

CARL BARRELED DOWN THE road, then slowed his pace so he wouldn't get stopped by a cop. At the closest gas station, he stopped and reported the break-in, then hung up without giving his name.

Then he drove a few blocks away, continuing down a residential street as he considered what to do.

He'd gone looking for Sidney, and he hadn't found her. Maybe she was at Luke's office.

He didn't know where the guy worked, exactly, but he must be in the phone book.

What about the three men in business suits? They'd shown up at Sidney's house, so what was to stop them from going after Luke?

He tried to reason his way through the logic of the situation, which was not his strong suit. They'd come to Sidney's house, and they'd been able to figure out who she was because she worked for him. If they didn't have Luke's name, it would still be okay to try his house.

Or was that safe?

He didn't want to tangle with those guys. But maybe he had to take a chance on going to Luke's.

And maybe he should just get the hell out of town until all this blew over.

That scenario had a lot of appeal. Then he thought of what his father would say when he learned that Carl had spent a lot of money on a shipment of antiques, some of which were now lost or broken.

He shuddered.

He'd better get the damn box back or—

He swallowed the words "die trying." He wasn't willing to go that far.

The Big Z had told Luke to sit down at the computer and get busy.

Instead, he figured he could take the time to let Sidney

know what they were doing. Turning to her, he said, "I've got to do a Web search. I don't think it will take too long."

He knew she was trying to read his expression. "Okay."

"After that, we can talk."

"Okay."

Enough. You are wasting my time.

Give me a minute.

You have not learned who is in charge. I say, enough!

Luke's anger rose. *And I say—*

He never finished the thought. Coherence deserted him as words he couldn't understand reverberated in his head like a huge Chinese gong that had been struck with a massive hammer. His vision blurred, and at the same time, excruciating pain jolted through his chest. He doubled over, gasping, fighting not to pass out.

Chapter Eight

Somehow Luke managed to reach out and catch himself against the wall before he toppled to the floor.

Sidney gasped and jumped forward. He knew her hand was on his arm, but he could barely feel it.

Or barely hear her voice as she asked anxiously, "Luke? Luke, what happened?"

He wasn't able to answer her. He was too busy fighting the dizzy feeling, the pain and the knowledge that it was all coming from within himself.

Stop! he screamed as iron bands circled his body, like a boa constrictor cutting off his air.

Finally, just when he was going down for the count, the pressure eased, and he took a cautious breath. It hurt, but not so much. Exerting the barest pressure, he let the air trickle out of his lungs.

"Luke? I'm going to call 911 if you can't answer me."

"Don't," he gasped out, then closed his eyes, praying for strength.

She knelt beside him. "What happened to you?"

He summoned enough breath to say, "Zabastian's angry with me."

She swore as she stared at him.

"Zabastian? I...I don't understand."

"He's angry...because I wasn't...going straight to the computer."

Her eyes narrowed as she kept her gaze on his face. And when she spoke, it was a warning to the warrior. "Zabastian, don't you ever do that to Luke again. He was trying to talk to me. You can't just control the two of us."

He heard his own voice grow more firm as Zabastian answered Sidney. "Getting the box back to its rightful owners is more important than your relationship."

"To you."

"To the world," the warrior bit out.

She scowled at him.

"I must do this job or die trying. Step out of my way."

"If you die, you won't be able to do it!" she shouted.

Luke felt Zabastian absorb that assessment. Maybe it would give the warrior a better grasp on reality.

Sidney kept her eyes on him as she stepped aside so that he could continue toward the home office.

He walked slowly, carefully, like he was suddenly a hundred years old.

What the hell did you do to me?

I squeezed your lungs.

And it doesn't hurt you?

Of course it does. But I have the discipline to with-stand it, the warrior's voice rang haughtily inside Luke's head. *And I applied only enough pressure to cause pain, not permanent damage.*

Thanks a bunch.

Luke wished he could sock the smug bastard in the

jaw. Only he'd be socking himself. Instead he had to settle for words.

Nice. So this is how you make sure the man you possess does your bidding? Punishment if he doesn't follow your orders.

I was hoping you would see the wisdom of the primary mission.

Luke made a rough sound. *The primary mission. You're the one who took the time to make love with Sidney.*

To control her.

Bull! You wanted her as much as I did. And you didn't have to spend any extra time lying in that cave with her curled up in your arms.

Zabastian cursed. The words were not in English, but Luke understood them as well as his native language.

That's very creative. Can you really do that with a temple rat?

Get to the computer.

Luke pressed his shoulder against the wall, his breath still shallow as he walked down the hall. He was aware that Sidney was right behind him, but he didn't spare the breath to speak to her. Zabastian had hurt him. Would he hurt her too if she tried to interfere?

I would not hurt her, the warrior answered inside his head.

And I'm supposed to trust you?

I do not lie.

Luke firmed his lips. There was no use arguing. He'd help the bastard find the Moon Priests, and that would be the end of it.

The end of it?

A little seed of doubt flickered inside his head. He'd

thought he caught something way below the surface of the warrior's thoughts.

But it evaporated as they kept walking to the end of the hall where Ginny and Tom's home office was located.

The computer sat on the desk, a computer he knew very well because he had built it. Sitting down, he booted the machine, then used one of the desktop icons to get into the Internet.

Now what?

I must open my mind to the machine.

Luke snorted.

"What?" Sidney asked.

"He's going to commune with the machine."

He could hear Sidney make some kind of comment, something that was better not to examine too closely.

The warrior ignored her. Luke could feel the man's concentration focusing as he stroked his fingers lightly over the keyboard, and Luke felt him connecting with the computer in a way that should have been impossible. It was like he was sending his mind into the chips that ran the processor—and from there into the World Wide Web.

Luke was an expert at searching the Web. But that was when he knew what he was looking for. In this case, he was sure that putting "Moon Priests" into a search engine wouldn't get him very far.

With no other option, he surrendered to the warrior, letting him use Luke's skill in ways he hadn't known existed, sorting through information with superhuman speed, probing and rejecting.

Luke felt like he was in the backseat of a speeding truck, with no control over where they were going, and knowing they might crash at any minute. He was pretty sure that too much of this high speed searching might give him a stroke. But he prayed it would be over soon and hung on as best he could.

The warrior paused at a Web site on "Crystal Children."

What's that? Luke asked as he scanned a few paragraphs.

The site seemed to be describing special children born in the past few generations. Children who could change the world because their abilities were beyond those of ordinary men and women.

It is very interesting. Perhaps you are one of them.

Me? How?

We do not have time for it now, the warrior said, and they sped on again.

Finally another Web address leaped into Luke's consciousness, and he typed it into the browser.

The screen went black and Luke cursed. Then it brightened again as a message came up.

"This site is password protected. Entrance is only for subscribers."

Now what? Luke asked.

A VAN, WHOSE NAME ON THE side advertised a local cleaning service, pulled up in front of Sidney's apartment. Two men in gray coveralls got out, carrying some cases with equipment. They checked the address, then walked around the side of the building.

But they stopped short when they saw the broken sliding glass door. One of the men spoke into an almost invisible microphone clipped to the lapel of his coveralls. "There's been a break-in here," Hunter Kelley said.

He, Dan Cassidy and Nick Vickers had all watched the surveillance tapes from the importer's building, and had seen the three men in the hallways and the garage. Too bad the cameras hadn't been in Peterbalm's office.

The shoot-out in the garage had been riveting. It was clear that only McMillan's quick thinking and Sidney's bravery had gotten them out alive.

"You think it's the same guys?" Dan asked from inside the van, where he was keeping watch.

"Either them or somebody connected."

"And it's tied to Peterbalm's importing stolen antiques," Nick added.

"Probably," Dan agreed. "So be careful," he added. He didn't usually go along on Light Street covert ops, but because his wife had first been contacted by Sidney Weston, he'd insisted on being on the scene when they searched her apartment.

Hunter was the most experienced of the trio. He had worked for Randolph Security and its sister enterprise, the Light Street Detective Agency, for over ten years, since his wife Kathryn Kelley had sprung him from a secret army unit grooming him for a suicide mission to the Middle East.

The third member of the team, Nick Vickers, was a vampire who had joined the Light Street group the year before. For obvious reasons, he worked mostly at night.

Hunter and Nick eyed the glass and each other. "Do we go in?" Hunter asked.

"Affirmative," Nick answered.

Both men set down their toolkits and gloved up. Hunter pulled out the sidearms stashed in one of the deep pockets of his coveralls and held the weapon in a two-handed grip. Nick relied on his vampire reflexes as he entered the apartment through the ruined door.

The place was a mess. Somebody had pulled out drawers, turned over furniture and yanked books from the shelves. Even the refrigerator and freezer stood open. Their contents spilled on the middle of the floor.

Hunter made a rough sound. "Someone wanted to trash this place."

"I'm betting they didn't find the box," Nick answered.

The two operatives proceeded into the apartment, where every room had been savaged.

Hunter was in the bathroom, looking at the medications dumped into the tub, when Dan Cassidy's voice came over the microphone again.

"Somebody must have called the cops. They just pulled up in front of the building. Get the hell out of there. I'll meet you on the other side of the woods."

Nick rushed toward the back of the apartment, moving at a vampire speed that Hunter couldn't hope to equal.

Over the microphone, Dan cursed. "One of them's going around the side."

"Bloody hell," Nick muttered, speaking in the vernacular that had been in vogue when he'd been a young man back in England:

Grim-faced, Hunter burst through the door and pounded into the woods.

They were too late to make a clean getaway.

"Police. Stop or I'll shoot," a voice rang in the night.

Hunter wished he had Nick's night vision. Ducking low to make himself a smaller target, he ran into the woods, brambles catching against his pant legs as he ran.

When the top of his head collided with a low tree limb, he cursed.

Behind him, he heard more than running feet. A sudden wind had kicked up, and was pretty sure that Nick had circled back, probably invisible to the officer pounding along in back of Hunter.

Once again, the cop shouted a warning. "Stop or I'll shoot."

No can do, Hunter thought. Not when he was going to end up at the nearest station house trying to explain what they'd been doing in Sidney Weston's apartment.

Behind Luke, Sidney made a small sound. "We can't get in."

"Not yet," he answered. It wasn't Luke speaking. The warrior replied with a kind of confidence that Luke wished he possessed.

Or maybe not. This guy's tendency to rush off half-cocked had almost gotten them killed.

Quiet, the warrior's voice spoke inside his head. *I must concentrate.*

Aye aye, sir. Luke stopped talking abruptly when he felt the warrior narrow his focus.

He picked up a crystal that lay on the desk beside the computer and turned it in his hand.

"What are you doing?" Sidney asked.

"Meditating," he said in a slow, even voice that was barely a whisper. "Let me focus."

Zabastian continued to play with the crystal as Luke closed his eyes, shutting out the world, cooperating as best he could with the man who was running the show.

At least at this moment in time, he couldn't help admire the warrior's iron will and the depths of his concentration.

Luke had never been one for meditation, but he recognized what Zabastian was doing. He was going into a deep trance that would be impossible for most people.

He felt his consciousness alter, felt himself disappear into a land where few men could follow.

In his perception, he seemed to be walking in a beautiful garden, with flagstone paths wandering through beds of pastel flowers. Was the peaceful and soul-satisfying scene from the warrior's imagination, or was this a real place he had visited?

He let the man's feet carry him along, into another area. Now they were in an herb garden, and he trailed his fingers against the leaves of the plants, the scents wafting up toward him. At the same time, he knew that in the real world, one of his hands gripped the crystal and the fingers of the other hand brushed against the letters and numbers of the keyboard. That was part of the process, too.

The garden and the keyboard were one—in some mysterious part of the universe where humans could never travel, except with the power of their minds.

Luke was along for the walk. His lips curved into a smile as numbers and letters formed in his mind.

He touched each of them on the keyboard, committing them to memory in the right order. 43Light.

His eyes blinked open, and he stared at the screen.

"Did you just type 43Light?" Sidney whispered.

"Yes."

"That's the address where my friends work," Sidney said.

He didn't know why that had turned into the password, but it had done the trick. Before they could discuss it further, a circle appeared in the center of the screen. The word above it said, "Enter." Only it wasn't in English— or any language he had ever seen. The letters weren't Roman or Greek or Cyrillic. They were something much older. A language that had originated on the Indian sub-continent thousands of years ago.

He moved the cursor to the button on the screen and clicked the mouse. Suddenly he was past the first screen and into the Web site—not that it would have done Luke McMillan any good.

The words that marched across the screen were written in the ancient language that had appeared over the button.

"What's that?" Sidney whispered.

"Let me read it."

"You can read that?"

"Not on my own," Luke answered. "But the Big Z can."

"That's the language the Moon Priests speak?"

"That's their native language. Yes."

HUNTER POUNDED INTO THE woods, the cop close behind him. The officer wasn't catching up, but he had a gun, and he was fully capable of using it.

Hunter thought of reports in the paper when an innocent man had been gunned down by the law. He hoped the guy didn't get a clear shot at him.

Seconds after the thought surfaced, he heard a cracking noise, and a bullet whizzed past his ear. He changed his path, hoping that the trees would block him better.

Then from behind him, the sound of the wind rose higher, shaking the leaves on the trees.

In the next second, the cop gasped out something that Hunter couldn't hear, then shouted, "What the hell?"

Hunter kept going. He had a good idea of what had happened, and the assumption was confirmed when Nick came abreast of him, not even breathing hard.

Hunter gasped out, "Thanks, buddy."

"Nothing to it."

"Did you hurt him?"

"I came up behind him and pushed him over. He knocked the air out of his lungs when he hit the ground. And, uh, I snatched the gun out of his hand while he was going down so he wouldn't hurt himself."

Hunter didn't spare the breath to ask another question. The van had appeared on the street at the other side of the woods. Only, thanks to technology developed by the labs at Randolph Security, the lettering on the side had morphed into something else.

It was now a delivery van from a flower shop in Towson.

The back door opened, and Hunter and Nick scrambled in, Nick taking up the rear to make sure his friend made it in safely. Nick had lived over a hundred and fifty years on his own resources, with no companions, feeling apart from the human race. Once he'd learned that the Light Street men and women wanted to be his friends, he'd become fiercely loyal to them.

In the short time he'd been with them, they'd come to rely on his special talents. Like the amazing speed and stamina that no mere mortal could match.

He snapped the door closed as Dan drove away.

"How many cop cars showed up?" Hunter asked.

"Two," Dan answered. "I guess a neighbor realized something was wrong."

"The apartment was a mess," Nick said. "I'm sure they were looking for that box and they didn't find it."

"From what Sabrina said, Sidney would have sense enough not to go home."

"And she's got protection. She's with that warrior," Nick added.

"You believe the warrior part?"

He laughed. "As much as I believe in vampires."

Dan nodded. "You have more experience than we do in foreign travel. You ever heard of anything like the Moon Priests?" he asked.

"No."

"I Googled them," Dan said. "I didn't find anything."

"Not surprising," Hunter answered. "It seems they go to great lengths to stay hidden."

"So did you come up with any clues about who wrecked Sidney's apartment?" Dan asked.

"Maybe they're working for the owner of the box," Hunter said.

"Not if Sidney's right about the Moon Priests. This doesn't look like what a bunch of priests would do."

"One thing we know," Nick added. "Whoever did it was mad as hell."

SIDNEY WATCHED AS LUKE read the words on the screen. She concentrated on the pictures: a mountain shrouded in mist, the moon shining through the clouds, a drop of rain glistening on a leaf.

"What does it say?" she asked.

"It's for Zabastian."

"How did they know you'd find the Web site?

"They couldn't be sure. But they were hoping I would be able to do it."

"And?"

"They want to know if the box is safe."

"How do you tell them?"

"See this button?" He pointed to one of the small rectangles on the left side of the screen. "Apparently that means 'get in touch with us.'"

"How could an ancient cult use the Web and e-mail?"

The man at the computer raised one shoulder. "They change with the times. You don't expect them to be chipping stuff out of stone—do you?"

That was more like what she'd expected from Luke. But she had to assume Zabastian knew what he was doing—with some borrowed expertise from Luke.

When he moved the cursor to that location and clicked, a blank e-mail message board appeared.

He began to type rapidly. The words seemed to be in the same language that had appeared on the Web site. Somehow the keyboard was magically producing the strange symbols.

"What are you saying?"

He kept his focus on the screen and the keyboard. "That I have the box and I will wait for instructions from the Master of the Moon."

He pressed "Send," and she waited to see what would happen. Only a few seconds later, a message came back.

Again, the words were unintelligible to Sidney.

Luke translated. "We are grateful that you have recovered our property."

"If they're so grateful," Sidney interjected, "ask them how the box got to Peterbalm Associates."

Chapter Nine

Carl Peterbalm drove around the block again. He'd heard that Luke ran his operation from a garage at the back of his property, but he'd never been here.

As far as he could tell, nobody had staked out the place.

As he walked toward the office, he saw that it was pretty dinky. Probably he'd be better off finding another computer expert.

On the other hand, McMillan had been willing to take the contract for pretty cheap.

Maybe he'd decided to supplement his income with robbery.

Carl was still thinking that Luke and Sidney had stolen the box and now the guys who played rough were after them.

He stopped down the block and waited for fifteen more minutes. When he decided it was safe, he slipped out of the car and walked back to the McMillan office. He found the door locked and broke the knob with a rock.

Inside, Carl fumbled for the switch and turned on the overhead light, illuminating worktables laden with computer parts. He noticed a filing cabinet and started riffling through the folders.

He'd have thought this guy would store everything in his computer. But apparently he wanted paper backup like most other people.

When Carl hit McMillan's client list, he looked through the entries. Some were for small businesses, others private residences. That sent Carl's mind working. Maybe one of those people would be willing to put up Luke and Sidney.

He folded the sheet of paper and slipped it in his pocket, then exited the garage, closing the door behind him.

THE INTRUDER HAD THOUGHT he was being careful, but he was an ordinary man and one who hadn't been trained in covert operations. Smith, Brown and Jones were much more adept at the covert skill.

After striking out at Sidney's, they'd used the special equipment they'd brought along to trace Luke's cell phone to his address.

They had arrived at the McMillan residence twenty minutes before this man and started scouting the area, preparatory to approaching the garage from three different directions.

But just before they'd climbed out of the car, the man had come hurrying up the sidewalk.

"He's looking for the computer guy."

They watched him go in, then watched him come out again a few minutes later.

"He's still in a hurry. He didn't find the man or the woman," Brown said.

"But his steps are purposeful. He thinks he knows where to locate them."

"You hope," Smith whispered.

They waited until the intruder had returned to his car, climbed in, and driven off. Then they eased out of their own parking space and followed with their lights off.

LUKE TYPED IN THE QUESTION Sidney had asked, and the answer came back almost at once.

He turned to her and said, "The items were smuggled into the country in a shipment of stolen antiques."

Sidney sucked in a sharp breath. "I was afraid of something like that."

"Those men stole the box?"

"No. They have been tracking it down. They almost found it in France. Then it shipped out with the Peterbalm consignment. Apparently everything in the cargo boxes was hot."

"Oh great."

Another message came through. "The Grand Master wants us to bring the box to them."

"When?"

"He'll give us instructions."

"Okay."

Luke leaned back in the chair, looking worn-out. He'd been transacting the warrior's business for hours.

"Now what?" Sidney asked.

"We have to wait until they give us the location of the temple."

"Why?"

"Because…" He stopped and thought. "Because it is not always in the same place."

"How could that be?"

He shrugged. "They hide the temple."

"How can it move around?"

"By utilizing an alternate space-time continuum."

"Glad I asked."

"Few people would understand it."

"Do you?"

He huffed out a breath. "No." After a few seconds, he turned and looked at Sidney. "I'm sorry you got caught in all of this."

"It wasn't your fault. Carl Peterbalm should have been more careful."

"Probably he thought it was a fantastic deal."

"If the deal was that good, he should have been suspicious." She sighed. "He's a jerk."

When they exhausted the subject of Carl Peterbalm, Luke shifted in his seat, looking like he was feeling awkward.

So was Sidney. They'd known each other for six months and hadn't managed to get close, although she knew they'd been attracted to each other. But a couple of hours ago, they'd made wild, frantic love. She longed to ask if he was having second thoughts about that, but she couldn't get the words out.

She turned and looked out the window into the night. She wanted to tell Luke that the password had been a sign that they should contact the Light Street Detective Agency, but she suspected he'd just veto the plan again.

When she said, "Let's try to relax while we're waiting," she could see some of the tension melt out of Luke's shoulders. "I think I saw some hot chocolate down in the pantry. How does that sound?"

"Good. But I need to stay at the computer, in case I get e-mail."

"I'll go fix the chocolate."

He gave her a long look, all business again. "Are you going to make any phone calls?"

"No."

"Or leave?

She shook her head.

"How do I know?"

"Because I want you to trust me," she whispered.

He answered with a tight nod.

She hurried down the stairs to the kitchen. She could have been lying to him, of course. But she wasn't. She wanted to call Sabrina, but she wasn't going to do it unless she could persuade Luke it was the right thing to do.

Instead, she made the hot chocolate, and was back in the office in less than four minutes.

"Nothing yet?" she asked.

He shook his head.

She handed him the mug, and he smelled the aroma. When he took a cautious sip, his face registered surprise. She knew the reaction came from Zabastian, not Luke.

"You have wonderful foods here," he said.

"How is it that you keep acting surprised at stuff like that? I mean, about things that Luke knows perfectly well."

"It is ordinary to Luke. But not to Zabastian."

She held up the cup. "This kind is made from a mix. Maybe I'll get a chance to fix you the real thing."

Luke grinned at her. "It's not just Zabastian. Actually, I've never had the real thing either."

"My mom used to make it for a treat. Dad would build

a fire in the fireplace, and we'd sit around watching the flames and drinking the chocolate."

"That makes a nice picture," he said wistfully.

"My apartment doesn't have a fireplace. But I have cocoa powder. Next time, I'll make that for you." She stopped short, wondering if there was going to be a next time.

Luke's expression told her he was thinking the same thing.

Clearing her throat, she said, "I'd like to talk to Luke for a while."

The man across from her nodded. Then his face took on a subtle change that she'd grown to recognize, and she knew that Zabastian was sinking into the background, giving her and Luke space, if not exactly privacy.

She rotated her cup, watching the marshmallow spin around and feeling awkward. If anyone had told her she'd be in this situation, she wouldn't have believed them.

"What's swirling around in your head?" Luke asked.

"I'm that obvious?"

"Yes."

"A lot of things." Before she could stop herself, she said, "Like for example, I'm hoping you don't assume I'm the kind of woman who has one-night stands."

"That's not what it was!"

"Care to elaborate?"

He ran his hand over his face. "Maybe that's all you want out of it."

"Are you trying to push me away?" she challenged.

"Are you trying to back away?" he countered.

She made a frustrated sound. "No. But we got into this

relationship backward. I've never slept with somebody first, then tried to get to know him better." She stopped abruptly, wondering how that sounded to him. "I'm sorry. I'm embarrassed, so that might have come out wrong."

"You have nothing to be embarrassed about," he said quickly.

"I could have been so embarrassed that I walked away from you."

"Don't!"

The way he said it gave her confidence that perhaps they could get through the awkward part and work their way into something meaningful. "So, maybe we can get to know each other better. I mean me and Luke," she qualified. "I'd like to know more about you."

"Like what?"

"You're from Baltimore, right?"

"I'm from the wrong side of the tracks. My grandmother raised me after my parents split up," he said immediately. "She was a secretary at a marine shipping company."

She heard herself laugh. "That's a real icebreaker. Is that how you start conversations in bars?"

"I'm not much for picking up women in bars."

"Good. That's not where I want to meet men."

He shifted in his seat. "I just didn't want to give you any false impressions about me or my background."

CARL PETERBALM TURNED ON the car light and consulted the list that he'd taken from McMillan's office. He'd already tried two customers who might have taken in Sidney and the computer guy. Now he was going to try the third most likely. The house had risen to the top of the list, because the last people had told him the Hanovers were out of town.

As far as Carl was concerned, that made their house a grade-A hiding place.

He set out for the house feeling a lot more optimistic about getting his property back. If he could clear this whole thing up in the next couple of days, his dad wouldn't have to know a thing about how he'd messed up.

"OKAY. I'LL BE HONEST, TOO." Sidney gave Luke a challenging look. "A little while ago, I was thinking that distancing myself from you would solve my problem. Now I'm thinking that would be the coward's way out. How do you feel about us?"

"That's certainly a direct question."

"Do you want to put distance between us?" she persisted.

He shifted in his seat. "No."

She'd been holding her breath. Now she let the air trickle out of her lungs. "Good."

He took a sip of chocolate, then looked at her. "I liked you the first time I met you. I wanted to get to know you better. But I thought you wouldn't be interested in me."

"Why not?"

"You're still being pretty direct."

"I figure we've been in a pressure cooker and living through the equivalent of six months together in the past few hours. That gives us the ability to cut through a lot of ordinary stuff."

"Yeah."

"But we still don't understand each other. I'm guessing you don't know how much I admired you."

His features registered shock. "You admired me?"

"I asked around about you. I knew you came from a...disadvantaged background."

"And I didn't go to college," he added, putting that piece of information squarely between them.

"Right. And I did. And to give you the short version of my life, I had loving parents who made a good home for me in Catonsville. Dad was a pharmacist for a drugstore chain. And Mom was a teacher's aide in an elementary school. I got a partial scholarship to the University of Maryland—Baltimore County. I majored in fine arts, and I had big dreams of what I was going to do with my life. I wanted to start my own business, but my dad died while I was in college."

"I'm sorry."

"Mom is living on the widow's portion of his pension, which is just enough for her to get by." She heaved in a breath and let it out. "I had to go to work for a jerk like Carl Peterbalm because I had debts to pay. So here I am—two years out of college, and I haven't done any of the things I want to. But you have. You worked for a computer repair company and learned the ropes before you started on your own. You started building computers for people—selling prompt and efficient service along with the machines. That's how you compete against the big office supply stores that offer mass-produced machines at discounts."

His expression turned bemused. "You sure know a hell of a lot about me!"

"Because I was interested. Betty Custer and I got to talking about you."

"Betty went to school with me."

"I know. And she said you were kind of wild." She laughed. "She thinks it was because you had low self-esteem."

The color in his cheeks had heightened. "Nice of her."

"It was true, wasn't it? That's why you went out of your way to be a tough guy in school and why you wouldn't have asked me out."

His face contorted. "Okay, yeah."

"So you didn't know I envied you."

"For what?"

"Doing what I couldn't do. Working for yourself instead of a guy you hate."

"I work for Peterbalm."

"You know what I mean. You don't work for him all the time. You accepted him as a client. That was your choice. Probably you don't like him, but you see him as a stepping-stone."

He nodded.

"I'll bet your grandmother is really proud of you."

"She was. She smoked all her life, and she died of lung cancer last year."

"I'm sorry."

"She had a hard life. I tried to make things better for her. She wanted to die in her own home, and I was able to get a hospital bed for her and arrange nursing care."

"That must have been expensive."

He shrugged. "I wanted her to know how much I loved and respected her."

"I'm sure she did."

"I gave her a hard time when I was a teenager," he said quickly. "Some other tough guys in the neighborhood and I used to boost cars and go joyriding."

"I got in trouble, too."

"Oh yeah?"

"Hooking class with my girlfriends."

"Why did you do it?"

"It was cool. And so was smoking. I'm lucky I hated those little pieces of nicotine in my nose."

"Yeah. Very lucky."

He tipped his head to the side, studying her, and she struggled to hold her gaze steady.

"I don't see you as being a conformist."

"I'm smarter now."

He nodded, then finished the last of the chocolate in the cup. "I should practice some of my exercises," he said.

"Exercises?"

"Zabastian says my body isn't as limber as it should be. He says I'm not prepared for trouble."

"Are we expecting trouble?" she asked, hearing her voice go a little high.

"I hope not. But I should be ready."

"You want me to go somewhere else?"

"You can stay."

She pushed the desk chair into a corner and sat down, watching as Luke slipped off his shoes and socks before dimming the light in the room. Only the desk lamp provided a small amount of illumination as he stood in the center of the rug with his arms hanging at his sides.

His lips moved and he spoke words she couldn't hear as he raised his hands above his head before folding in the middle, then dropping to his hands and feet in a posture that she recognized as a yoga pose. Downward facing dog.

He went through more yoga moves like the salutation

to the sun. She'd taken some classes and seen it done before but never as fast as Luke was doing it.

She watched as he slipped easily into a zone where he was far away from her and from the world.

Then he went into some of what she knew were the warrior poses.

He seemed to be operating on another plane of existence—until the doorbell rang. As the sound reverberated through the house, he snapped instantly back into the real world.

She and Luke stared at each other.

"Are we expecting company?" she whispered.

"I don't know."

He moved to the window and looked down toward the front door, but the view was obscured by the porch roof.

Luke pushed down the arm of the desk lamp so that the light in the room was barely visible.

"I'll keep watch on the street. You slip downstairs and into the dining room. Look out the window and see if you can tell who's on the porch."

The doorbell rang again.

Sidney hurried downstairs and into the darkened dining room. When she looked out the window, she saw a bulky man standing on the porch. Because the light was off, it took her several seconds to recognize him. It was Carl Peterbalm.

He was holding something in his hand, and she saw it was a flashlight. She jumped back, but maybe he had seen the movement in the darkness.

The beam zeroed in on the window. She saw Peterbalm's face register shock, then triumph.

"Sidney!" he shouted. "I see you in there. Let me in."

Chapter Ten

Sidney heard Luke pound down the steps. He grabbed her arm and was pulling her away from the door when three other men ran up the walk.

She gasped when she saw who they were—the men who had tried to kill them earlier.

They'd found her and Luke again. Or rather, Carl Peterbalm had found them, and the men had followed him.

As she watched, one of the men grabbed the importer and spun him around. Carl gasped as the man threw him to the ground.

One ran around to the back of the house, and the third one smashed the butt of his gun against the window glass. Luckily it was an old-fashioned storm window, so the gun butt only went through the outside pane. The man reached through the jagged glass and cried out as he sliced his arm.

It all happened with lightning speed. Luke was almost as fast. He grabbed Sidney's hand and hustled her back up the stairs.

As she ran, she managed to ask, "Why didn't they shoot?"

"Maybe they don't want to risk it in a residential neighborhood."

"People will hear the glass breaking."

"Not necessarily. These lots are big. That gives the Poisoned Ones privacy. I guess they think they've got us trapped and they can grab the box and get out of here before the cops come."

She was breathing hard as Luke dragged her down the hall to the computer room.

"We have to get the box to safety," he told her as they ran.

"But how? Where?"

When they reached the upstairs office, Luke hit a key that deleted the Web site where he'd been communicating with the Moon Cult. Then, without going through the shutdown procedure, he pressed the power button and the screen went blank. From downstairs, Sidney could hear sounds of breaking and entering. She looked wildly around. "What are we going to do? There's no way out of here. Are you thinking we can climb into the attic?"

"No. They are trained to think of every hiding place inside the house. We have to disappear."

He turned her toward him, then he set the box on the floor right beside them.

"We can hide. In the cave where I made love to you."

She stared up at him, trying to take that in. "But…"

The protest was cut off when his mouth came down on hers, swallowing whatever she had been going to say.

He spoke against her lips, his voice low and urgent. "Focus on me, Sidney. It won't work unless you and I are on the same wavelength."

Oh sure. He wanted to make her hot—when murderers were closing in on them?

Still, she tried to do as he asked because she knew it was their best chance. But she didn't have the same level of concentration as Luke when glass was breaking and doors were slamming.

"Stay with me, Sidney. Only me."

Luke gathered her to him, his lips moving over hers, and as he did, she felt some kind of bubble form around them. Her eyes were open, and she could still see the room, but now she was looking at it through a gauze-covered lens.

As her vision changed, the sounds from the rest of the house receded into the background.

"Focus on me, Sidney. Remember how good we are together."

Who had spoken to her—Luke or Zabastian?

She knew it was both of them. The man she had known for months and the warrior who had come roaring into her life.

As she gave him her total concentration, the room where they stood faded away. She could see the cave now—glimmering in the darkness, not quite solid but more real than the office where they had been standing.

It was a strange sensation. Somewhere outside their time bubble, she thought she heard at least one of the men rushing up the stairs toward them. She tensed, but Luke brought her back to him with the play of his lips and tongue and the stroke of his hands over her bottom.

The two images of reality still hung around her—the room and the cave—and she wondered if the two scenes were fighting for dominance.

Would the men still see them as dimly as she saw the room? Would they know where she and Luke had gone? Could they follow?

That question sent a shiver over her skin.

"We must leave. And quickly," Luke murmured against her lips.

That piece of news wasn't the idea spur to arousal. Yet she called on all the feelings of connection she had to Luke. As she trained her entire focus on him, the room faded out of her sight, and she and the man who held her in his arms were back in the cave where they'd made love.

The fire still flickered, although it had burned lower since they'd been here earlier. The bed of furs still waited in the corner, Luke's torn shirt still lay on the floor. And the wind still howled outside their refuge.

He breathed out a sigh. "Thank you for trusting me."

"Did I have a choice?"

"Not if you wanted to avoid getting killed."

MR. SMITH STOPPED IN THE doorway to the home office. Then, crossing to the computer, he put his hand on the metal casing. It was warm. Someone had been here. Probably the man and woman who had taken the box. At least, Peterbalm had seen someone he knew through the window.

Jones was in the basement, checking every hiding place. Brown was on the first floor.

Smith methodically went through the rest of the rooms on the upper story, but they were empty. And all the windows were closed and locked.

He looked above him for the entrance to the attic. After finding it in the middle of the hallway, he pulled a chair over, pushed up the panel and swung himself up, then used his flashlight to examine the dusty space. But he saw no one and no place where a person could hide, so he lowered himself to the floor again.

When he came back down to the first floor, the man named Peterbalm was lying unconscious on the living room rug.

"He had a list of clients with him," Brown observed.

"We should kill him," Jones said.

"No. He may have information."

"But we'll lose valuable time."

"The computer was warm," Smith told the others. "They can't be long gone."

"You think they saw us coming and got away?" Jones asked. "Or they saw Peterbalm and that was enough?"

"Peterbalm alerted them. But I think they saw us."

Smith stroked his chin, thinking. "I don't see how they disappeared…unless they used magic."

Jones's expression hardened. "You mean they're still here—but we can't see them?"

"Yes," the other man hissed. He looked around the living room. "I'll stay here. You take Peterbalm and keep going down his list—in case I'm wrong."

"You think it's wise to split up?" Brown asked.

Smith glared at him. "I don't like it. But I see no other option." He nodded at Peterbalm. "Tie him up and put him in the trunk of his car. Then use his car to go to the other places. If you have no success, come back." He looked at his watch. "In two hours."

LUKE FELT A SHIVER GO through Sidney's body and wished he hadn't felt compelled to talk about death.

What the hell was wrong with him?

Stupid question. The warning had come from the warrior. The guy had allowed Luke to be in charge of the conversation when they'd been drinking the hot chocolate, but Luke knew he wasn't the one who had taken them back to this place and time.

Is this a real place? he asked inside his head.

Not exactly.

You mean, we couldn't live here permanently?

You would not want to.

Thanks. How long can we stay?

A few hours.

Luke looked around.

It's the same cave.

But you haven't been to the interior. He reached for Sidney's hand and weaved his fingers with hers.

"Come with me. We're going farther back."

Zabastian led her through an opening in the back of the cave that Luke would have sworn wasn't there the first time they were here. They walked down a passageway where torches fixed to the walls provided flickering light.

He could feel the atmosphere getting warm and steamy, and he found out why when they stepped into another large room. In the center of this one was a hot spring, gushing out of the rocks and into a pool, then running down a channel that led into an underground passage.

Beside him, Sidney looked around in wonder.

"Was this here before?"

"I don't think so," Luke answered.

"Then how…"

"I think this cave comes from Zabastian's imagination, or maybe it's a collection of memories."

She made a frustrated sound. "I get the feeling you don't know for sure."

"No. But it's a good place to hide out."

She tipped her head and looked at him. "You're talking like Luke, but Zabastian brought us here."

"I think you can deal with me as one guy—Luke. Unless there's some reason for the Big Z to assert himself."

"Thanks. I think."

"Let's not waste time talking." Before she could answer, he set down the box on a rock ledge high above the water, then bent his head and rubbed his lips back and forth against hers, this time more softly, because they really did have time to enjoy this place. After all, hiding out wasn't an option, it was a necessity.

He sucked at her bottom lip, then slipped one hand under her shirt, sliding his fingers in delicious circles over her back, entranced by her soft skin. With more finesse than he'd managed the first time, he unhooked her bra and heard her breathing change.

He'd been ready to make love with her when he brought her here, but now the needy sound jolted up his arousal another notch.

He slid one hand down her spine again, then cupped the fullness of her bottom, pulling her more firmly against his erection.

The Luke McMillan part of him wanted to tell her he had fallen in love with her months ago. But he wasn't free to say it. Not when he knew that he had to deliver the box to the Moon Priests—or die trying.

He looked down so she wouldn't see the resigned expression that crossed his face, then shoved the thought to the back of his mind as he clasped Sidney's body against his. If he died, then he would take these moments with Sidney to heaven with him.

Greedily, he turned his full attention back to her. Putting a little distance between them, he reached out for the buttons on her borrowed blouse.

This time as he opened them, he was more careful not to tear them off. When the front of the shirt hung loosely, he bent his head, pressing his face between her breasts, then turning to kiss the inner curve of one full mound and then the other.

She clasped the back of his head in her arms, holding him against her. Smiling, he slid his mouth to one taut nipple and circled it with his tongue before sucking it into his mouth.

He was rewarded by Sidney's small gasp.

He switched to small kisses over her breast as he unsnapped her slacks, lowered the zipper and slicked the pants and her panties down her legs.

Without raising his head, he said, "Get me out of these jeans. They're killing me."

He heard her soft laugh, then felt her unbuckle his belt and lower his zipper.

He held his breath, willing her to reach inside and take him in her hand. When she did, he sighed out his pleasure.

"Lord, that's good," he told her, as she squeezed and stroked him. He knew he could only take so much of that focused attention, so he lifted her hand away from his erection, then shucked his jeans and undershorts.

She was still wearing her shirt, and he slid it off her shoulders and down her arms, tossing it onto the rocks.

Taking her hand, he led her to stone steps carved into the side of the pool.

As they descended hand in hand into the steamy water, she made a soft sound of pleasure.

"Nice."

"Oh yeah," he answered, testing his footing as he led her farther into the pool. With a grin, he dragged her down into the water, crouching beside her as she floated on the surface of the natural hot tub.

He kept one arm under her. With the other, he began to stroke her, enjoying the view of her floating body as he aroused her to a high peak of pleasure, bringing her to the edge of orgasm and then letting her settle.

"Luke," she gasped. "I need…"

"Yes." He lifted her in his arms, then set her on a narrow shelf that jutted from the side of the pool. Opening her legs, he moved between them so that he could easily thrust inside her.

She gasped as he entered her.

The water slowed his movements, inciting his need and yet governing the pace.

Standing in front of her, he had wonderful access to her body. He stroked her as he moved in and out of her, one hand on the spot where her pleasure centered and one hand caressing her breast.

He felt her inner muscles spasm, heard her gasp as she came undone for him.

As she clenched around him, he followed her over the edge, shouting in satisfaction as he absorbed the pleasure she gave him.

Then she was gathering him to her, holding on tightly, and he clung to her just as fiercely.

He held her for long minutes, feeling her head droop to his shoulder.

"I wish we could stay here," she murmured.

"For a little while," he answered.

"This isn't real life."

He lifted his head and looked down at her. "No."

She cuddled against him. Finally he pulled away and plunged into the water, submerging himself, then coming to the surface and floating the way she had earlier.

She leaned down to kiss him, and he reached up a hand to cup her head.

And somehow they got tangled up together. He went down, sputtering, then surfacing.

"Are you all right?"

"Um hum." He didn't know when they would be together again like this and he couldn't stand the thought of it ending, not yet. So he stood again, pulling the length of her slick body against his.

Clasping her close, he climbed out of the pool, then carried her to a dark corner of the cave where spongy leaves made a perfect bed. As he laid her down and began to kiss and caress her, he struggled to keep the feeling of desperation from the front of his mind. He'd told her this wasn't real life. Would they get a chance for that together? He prayed for the chance to build a life with her. But he knew deep in his heart that his prayers might not be answered. This might be the last time they would ever make love.

LYING IN THE TRUNK OF HIS own car with his hands bound and a gag wadded in his mouth, Carl Peterbalm feared the worst.

There was only one good thing about the situation. It was *his* car.

He'd woken up when the thugs were binding his hands and feet, and he'd still been groggy when they'd slapped him around and asked a bunch of questions. He'd told the truth—that he'd bought the shipment of antiques and that he didn't know where the hell the box had gone. He'd hoped they'd let him go. Instead, they'd carried him to the car. As soon as they had shut the lid, his whole life had flashed before his eyes.

He could easily die here. Only he wasn't going to let that happen, because he'd imagined this scenario for years.

Well, not exactly *this* scenario. Not three fierce, foreign-looking men driving around searching for an antique box.

They wanted the damn thing, badly. Which meant it was valuable. It looked like they'd picked up his trail when he was looking for Sidney and Luke.

Somehow, the two of *them* had escaped from the house and were on the loose again.

If the men didn't find Luke and Sidney soon, they'd work harder to get every scrap of information out of him. Then they'd kill him.

His only option was to get away before they opened the trunk again.

Sweat poured off his body, and he had to keep fighting off the panic attack that threatened to make his heart pound its way through the wall of his chest.

He struggled not to let the fear envelop him. If he gave in to it, he was dead. The men who had kidnapped him were good fighters, and smart, but they didn't know American vehicles the way Carl did.

He'd been a car buff all his life, and knew this model had an interior release button in the trunk. Worried about carjackings, he'd rigged up a sharp piece of metal hidden beside the left brake light.

Since the ride had begun, he'd maneuvered himself so that his hands were positioned against the sharp edge. Ordering himself to work slowly and carefully, he started sawing at the duct tape the kidnappers had used to bind his hands.

Not able to see what he was doing, he cut his wrist, and yelped at the jolt of pain. But he grit his teeth, changed the angle of his hands and kept working, because that was his only option.

When he'd cut through the tape, he pulled the gag from his mouth and gave a sigh of relief.

The car stopped then and he tensed, listening to traffic noises. As the vehicle jerked forward again, he figured they had only paused for a traffic light. After a few minutes the car stopped again, and the engine shut off. He could hear the men in front talking in some language he couldn't understand.

When the door opened, he held his breath, praying that they weren't coming for him. Apparently his luck was holding. He heard their footsteps receding up a sidewalk.

Carl took a steadying breath and told himself to stay calm. This might be his only opportunity to escape and he'd better not blow it.

But what if they were looking at the car and saw him climb out?

Because staying here meant pain and probably death, he had to take the chance on escape. Popping the lid, he held the edge so he could ease it up slowly, then peer out.

When he saw only cars and shrubbery, he slithered out of the trunk and closed it again so they wouldn't know he was gone.

Crouching beside one of the back tires, he peeked out, and his breath caught as he saw the men standing on the sidewalk in front of a house twenty yards away. They were talking to each other, thank the Lord, and not looking at the car.

Ducking low, he willed himself to steadiness, then ran into the traffic lane and across to the opposite sidewalk.

Turning the corner, he dove into some bushes, where he sat breathing hard and marveling that he'd really gotten away.

Or had he?

Afraid to move, he sat where he was, listening for the sound of his car engine and praying that the thugs didn't check the trunk.

When the car pulled away, he felt like he'd been born again.

So what should he do with that second chance at life?

He couldn't go home. They'd come looking for him. But maybe he could still find Sidney and Luke. They'd stolen his property, and he wanted it back. Only this time he was going to be a lot more careful, starting with arming himself.

LUKE AND SIDNEY STAYED IN the warm, wet cave for a few hours playing in the water again, then returning to the bed. Sidney lay peacefully in Luke's arms, but his mind was racing, trying to make plans for what might happen when they got back to her century.

Finally, it was impossible to hide the tension tightening his muscles.

"You're thinking we have to go back. And you're worried about it," she said.

He slicked his damp hair back from his forehead. "Yes."

He got up and found woven pieces of fabric folded on a rock shelf. Towels.

First he draped a towel over Sidney's shoulders. Then he lovingly used another towel on her damp hair, then combed his fingers through the silky strands.

"When the warrior first came to you, he wanted to put me in my place," she said in a soft voice as she moved her cheek against his middle.

"Yes."

"How does he feel now?"

"He…" Luke stopped and listened to the voice inside his head. "He understands that things have changed between men and women over the centuries. He understands that the two sexes are more equal in our world."

"Nice of him."

"He's changed," Luke said in a low voice.

"A kinder, gentler warrior?"

He laughed. "Yeah. We've both changed. The two of us have each learned from the other."

"But it's still…unsettling."

"Of course."

And this was one of those times. He longed to tell Sidney what making love to her had meant, but the silent voice of the warrior stopped him cold.

We do not need that complication.

I need it.

Later.

Will there be a later?

You know what we have to do.

He wanted to demand an answer, but the warrior wasn't giving him any guarantees. The silent exchange told him that until the box was returned to the Temple of the Moon, he could only show Sidney what he felt by his deeds. He—Luke McMillan. And also Zabastian, because he knew the warrior's feelings ran deep, too. Even if he wouldn't admit it,

He reached for her, held her for a while longer, until he could no longer delay.

As she pulled on her clothing, she said, "There's something I wanted to ask you. If the box is so important to the Moon Priests, why don't they keep it in the temple all the time?"

"Because the sanctuary is shielded from the world and the box would lose its power if it stayed locked up inside the temple walls."

"Inconvenient."

"Yes. They must send it out into the world to recharge."

"But if it gets too much energy, it explodes."

"Something like that."

"Why don't they fix the problem?"

"Because they cannot tamper with the delicate balance of the universe."

"You're going around in circles."

"That's not my fault. Neither you nor I have the ability to fully understand the power of the box."

"So we have to take it on faith?" she pressed.

"Yes." He looked toward the outer room of the cave. "We must go back.

"How do we know it's safe?"

"We can peek through and see."

"Like when we came here and we weren't one place or the other?"

"Yes," he answered as he picked up the box and headed for the front of the underground complex.

They walked back the way they'd come, around the fire and to the front entrance. Luke pulled the pelt aside that closed the door, and they both looked out into the valley below. As they watched, the scene faded, and the office came into view.

Sitting at the desk chair was one of the men who had first come to Carl Peterbalm's office. He was facing the door to the room, his features alert and an automatic weapon cradled in his lap.

Sidney stepped quickly back into the safety of the cave and turned to Luke, her eyes wide.

"What do we do?" she asked in a breathy voice.

"It looks like they left him there to guard the place."

"Or there could be more of them here," she murmured.

"I think the others are out looking for us. But I can't be sure."

She answered with a small nod, but the tension on her face betrayed her uncertainty.

He gave her a long look. He'd told Zabastian that women and men were equal here. And he'd thought that he'd gotten to know Sidney very well since the men had first burst into her office. But he hadn't expected a test like the one he was going to propose.

Chapter Eleven

Luke kept his gaze trained on Sidney's face. "The only way I can see getting out of this is to split up. If you go into the hallway and get his attention, I can come up behind him."

"Split up?" she murmured, obviously considering the implications. "Okay. But how do I get into the house without going through this doorway?"

He walked along the cave wall, running his hand along the roughened surface. "We can make another doorway here. That should put you in the hall."

"Just like that we can make another doorway?"

He answered quickly, "It's possible, if you believe it can happen."

"You mean this is like Neverland? Or maybe the Wizard of Oz?"

Luke silently shared the references with Zabastian. "I guess you could put it that way." He laughed, then felt his expression turn serious. "It could be dangerous. I mean, that guy is sitting with a gun in his lap. He could shoot you."

"Then he loses an informant. He has no idea where to find the box."

"True," Luke agreed. But he still didn't like it.

"Luke, you'd better open the doorway."

Hoping he wasn't just blowing smoke when he'd told Sidney to have faith, he ran his hand against the stone wall. After a few moments, he felt it give way slightly.

The solid rock started to thin, and as he stroked the rough surface, he began to see through, into the hallway of the house where they'd been hiding.

The area was clear, but his chest tightened as he thought about the danger to Sidney. "Are you sure?"

"It's our best chance. What do I have to do?"

His voice was strained as he spoke around the lump in his throat. "In a minute, you can step through the wall and go quietly down the hall. Then you call out, like you've been somewhere else and just arrived back at the house."

"Okay."

He reached for her and pulled her to him, clasping her tightly, and she clung to him for a long moment, then pushed away and turned back to the cave wall. It was almost totally obliterated now, and they could see into the hallway.

"Is this Luke's plan or Zabastian's?" she murmured.

"Both of us. We're working together."

He watched her step through then. He wanted to keep watching, to make sure she was safe, but he had to get into position behind the Poisoned One. So he hurried to the cave entrance and pulled back the pelt.

"Luke? Are you still here, Luke?" Sidney called from the end of the hall.

As the man jumped to his feet, gun in hand, and charged toward the hallway, fear surged through Luke.

He wanted to shout a warning to Sidney, but he knew surprise was his best advantage. He said a quick prayer, then reached through the opening and set down the box before throwing himself at the man's back.

The Poisoned One heard something behind him and half turned. But it was too late for the attacker to make it all the way around. Luke tackled him, throwing him to the carpet before he reached the doorway.

The guy cried out in surprise and went flat on his face, but he recovered quickly, twisting around so he could get his weapon into position.

The two of them struggled, each using their martial arts training.

From the corner of his vision, Luke saw Sidney leap into the room. He wanted to shout at her to stay back, but he couldn't spare the breath or the concentration.

The man gave him a head butt that made his own head feel like a Chinese gong.

He retaliated with a nerve pinch that should have put the guy out of commission, but he'd apparently been taught how to slip far enough from his opponent's grasp to neutralize the technique.

Sidney flew by, heading for the desk.

Then, in a flash of movement, she brought her arm down.

Luke saw the heavy glass paperweight in her hand just before it thudded against the man's skull, and he went down.

"Good work," he said to Sidney as he rolled away from the thug, out cold on the floor.

"Are you all right?" she demanded.

"Yes. Are you?"

"Yes."

"Let's make sure he can't attack again." He reached down and handed Sidney the gun. "Keep him covered."

She did as he asked, while he riffled through the desk drawers and found a roll of strapping tape. After lifting the man into the chair, he wound the tape around his upper body, securing him in place.

Then he taped his wrists to the chair arms and his legs to the horizontal pieces that held the wheels. By the time he finished, the Poisoned One was stirring.

He lifted his head and glared at Luke. "Where were you?"

"I'll ask the questions. When are your friends coming back?"

The man pressed his lips together.

"There are ways to make you talk."

"You won't use them in front of her," the man said with confidence.

"Don't count on it."

Luke itched to slap him across his smug face. He knew that striking his opponent's flesh would give a feeling of satisfaction, but that was all he'd get out of it.

He glanced toward the computer. He wanted to boot it up and see if the Master of the Moon had sent him the location of the temple. Two things stopped him: he didn't want the Poisoned One anywhere near the message, and he knew that staying would waste precious time.

Instead, he stuffed a gag in the man's mouth and taped it in place, then picked up the box where he'd set it on the floor. He and Sidney were on their way out of the office when the sound of the front door opening and closing stopped them in their tracks.

"Smith?" someone called from the floor below.

The man in the chair made a muffled sound as he tried to respond.

"Smith?" the question came again.

When the captive didn't answer, two sets of footsteps come pounding up the steps. Luke knew it wasn't the Hanovers coming home to check their e-mail.

Two men leaped into the room. Sizing up the situation quickly, one of them grabbed Sidney and knocked the gun out of her hand. It hit the rug with a dull thud as he held her against his chest and his own gun against her head.

The other trained his weapon on Luke.

"Turn over the box or I'll kill the woman," the Poisoned One said in a deathly calm voice.

Luke hesitated. If he gave him the box, he knew that he and Sidney would be dead moments later.

Let me have full control, Zabastian shouted inside his head.

The last time you had full control, you almost got us killed.

This time you will be killed, if you do not do it.

In the hours since Zabastian's spirit had come shooting out of the box, Luke had gotten more comfortable with the joint custody of his body. Now, in a desperate act of faith, he opened his mind fully to Zabastian, allowing the warrior to take the helm. As he did, the world seemed to go into fast forward. Or maybe it was Luke who leaped out of the space-time continuum into some parallel reality.

Moving like a whirlwind, he hurled the box between the two men.

Their faces registered shock, and they both made a grab for the precious object, their attention momentarily diverted from Sidney and Luke.

As they took their eyes off of him, he leaped forward, knocking away the gun trained on Sidney, then whirled to kick out a foot, catching the other man in the balls.

The attacker doubled over, and Luke brought the side of his hand down on the man's neck.

"Down, Sidney," he shouted.

Sidney ducked, throwing the other man off balance, as Luke whirled back around, catching the assailant in the face with his elbow. The man made a gurgling sound as he sank to the floor.

Sidney looked on in amazement as he gave each of the men another solid kick.

"How…how…"

"I let the Big Z take over," he answered as he strode into the hall and picked up the box, turning it in his hand, making sure that it was all right.

Other than a slight chip out of one corner, it looked the way it had when he'd first picked it up.

He looked back at the men who had attacked them. He should shoot the bastards. But the thought of Sidney's watching him do it curdled his stomach.

Before he could make a decision, the sound of sirens came drifting toward them through the night air.

"Do you think they're coming here?" Sidney whispered.

"Don't know."

But as the sound grew louder, he changed his mind. "Yeah, I think they are. We'd better split."

He grasped the box against his chest with one hand

and held on to Sidney with the other, hurrying her down
the steps. By the time they reached the first floor, he
could see patrol cars pulling to the curb outside the
house.

"Oh hell."

Sidney stared wide-eyed through the window. "What
do we do now?"

"Get out the back way, I hope."

They sprinted for the rear of the house and ran into
the backyard, just as a cop came around the side of the
residence.

Luke pulled Sidney into the shadows, praying that the
officer hadn't seen them. When the man kept going
toward the back door, Luke breathed out a small sigh. He
led Sidney along the stockade fence screening off the
alley and then through the gate.

The alley was clear, and he ushered her across. But
before they reached the other side, a cop car pulled into
view.

Sidney made a strangled sound. Luke kept his hand
firmly on hers, leading her into the backyard opposite his
friend's house.

Immediately, a large Doberman started barking.

Luke cursed and thrust the box into Sidney's hands.
As the dog came toward him, snapping and snarling, he
went down on his haunches.

"Good boy. I know you're defending your property.
Good boy."

The dog stopped snarling and looked at him with dark
eyes. Luke held out his hand, letting the animal sniff him.

"Good boy," he repeated.

The dog made a chuffing sound, and Luke patted him

on the head. He'd always been good with animals. He had the feeling that the Big Z had the same talent.

Sidney had hung back.

"Come on," he murmured to her, and she made a wide circle around the large animal. They had almost reached the end of the yard near the house when a powerful flashlight struck them in the back.

"Police. Halt."

In response to the menacing voice, the Doberman rushed to the back fence and started barking again, then snapped menacingly at the officer, who took a quick step back.

"Good dog," Luke whispered.

Taking advantage of the diversion, he hurried to the gate at the other end of the yard, and they slipped between the houses, then across the street and through the next backyard.

Another police siren sounded in the distance.

"They're all over the place." She turned toward Luke. "We've done all we can by ourselves."

"You have a suggestion?"

"Yes. Call my friends from 43 Light Street. I know they'll help us."

"I don't know them."

"I do. They're absolutely trustworthy."

"We've broken the law."

"A lot of their clients have."

He stopped talking aloud, switching to an internal debate. Luke versus the warrior. Zabastian didn't want to trust anyone. Luke argued that they were running out of options and that the longer they stayed on the street, the more likely they'd end up in a jail cell. If they got arrested, the cops would take away the box.

I will kill them before I give up the box, Zabastian said.

You can't kill them. They're the authorities.

I bow only to the authority of the Master of the Moon.

You're not going to get to him unless you let me handle this. Where are you going to get a computer to get that e-mail? Are you going to break into another house?

Before Luke got an answer, Sidney asked him, "Remember the password that got you into the Moon Priest's Web site? 43Light. Don't you think they might be trying to tell you something?"

He huffed out a breath. "Okay, you can call them."

"Does Zabastian promise not to hurt anybody?"

"Yes," Luke snapped, hoping it was true.

Sidney reached for her phone and realized she had lost it somewhere along the way.

When she explained her problem, he looked up and down the street, then pointed toward the left. "Up there is a business area. We should be able to find a pay phone." He took her hand and started in that direction. "Walk normally."

"Yeah, sure. And what are we doing out at—" She stopped and looked around, blinking as though she was just taking in their surroundings. "It's morning. I guess we've been on the run all night."

"With a couple of interludes in that cave," he said, hearing the thick quality of his voice.

She took on a wistful look. He thought she was going to say something, and he waited with his heart pounding. But she apparently changed her mind about discussing the cave.

They walked close together up the street, a couple out for an early morning stroll, but both of them were on the lookout for the cops.

On the avenue, most of the businesses were still closed.

"There's a phone up by that alley," Sidney pointed out.

"A good location."

Luke fumbled in his pocket and came up with some change. While Sidney stepped to the phone booth, he scoped out the alley.

Sabrina answered on the first ring, which meant that she must have been sitting by the phone.

"Sidney?"

"Yes."

"Thank God. Are you all right?"

"Yes. We escaped from the bad guys. But the cops are also looking for us."

"Where are you?"

She gave the cross streets. "We're about 20 yards up the block, at the alley. We'll wait in there."

"Hunter Kelley and Jed Prentiss are standing by to pick you up."

"I remember them from parties at the Randolph estate."

"Good. I'll give them the location."

"Okay. Thanks. How long before they get here?"

"They're already on their way."

"Thanks," she said again, then hung up and gave Luke an "Okay" sign. He nodded from his place in the shadows.

She looked up and down the street, spying a coffee shop that had opened up. They hadn't eaten since last night, and coffee and a muffin would taste really good.

She was about to ask Luke if he had any more money when a car pulled to a stop beside the phone booth.

Hunter and Jed already?

She stared at the vehicle, trying to see who was driving.

Then she saw it was the diesel Mercedes that Carl Peterbalm had taken over from his father. It wasn't his usual set of wheels, but he drove it to work occasionally.

He pulled to the curb, jumped out of the car and came around to her side.

"Sidney," he said, his voice a mixture of triumph and anger. "I found you!"

"How?" she breathed.

"I've been driving around ever since…" He stopped and changed directions. "And here you are standing right out on the street. Weren't you supposed to be unpacking a shipment of antiques and making an inventory list?"

She felt her features harden. Crossing her arms, she said, "You know damn well I ran into some problems. You bought a consignment of antiques that you knew were stolen."

He blanched. "How…"

"You're the one who got us all into trouble."

Carl shook his head. "Don't try to change the subject. You left the office with a carved wooden box that belongs to me."

"Did I?" she asked.

"I want my property back," he said as he pulled a gun from under his jacket.

She gaped at him. She'd never seen Carl Peterbalm with a weapon, and the sight was scary.

"Carl, calm down," she managed to say. "I don't have it."

Carl's eyes were wild as he gestured toward Luke, who was still standing in the alley. "No. He's got it."

The box was clearly visible in Luke's hand.

"You can't have it," Luke said. "It's stolen property, and it doesn't belong to you."

"Or you either. But I went through hell because of that thing and I want it back."

Sidney could barely believe her eyes. In all the time she'd worked for Carl Peterbalm, she'd never seen him act like this. He might be mean and petty and he might have sexually harassed her, but he had never seriously threatened anyone with violence.

Luke's voice was calm and even. "I'm taking it back to its rightful owners."

Carl snorted. "You expect me to believe that? You're going to sell it to the highest bidder."

"*You* might. I'm going to take it back where it belongs."

It seemed that Carl wasn't capable of listening, and his eyes had taken on a maddened look that told her he had tipped over the edge. "Hand it over before you get hurt."

Still, she had absorbed Zabastian's value in the time they'd been together. No way was she going to hand over the Moon Priests' property to Carl Peterbalm.

Raising her chin, she answered, "No."

"You're making a mistake." Carl's voice rose an octave. "I'm in the right here. You've taken my property. Those men almost killed me because of that damn box, so I know it's valuable. I'm through talking to you. Hand it over."

"Carl, listen to me." As she spoke, she took a step forward.

"Stay away from me before you get hurt." When he swung the gun toward her, she froze.

Luke took advantage of the opening and leaped forward.

As he charged, Carl fired the gun. At point-blank range, it would have been hard to miss a man right in front of him.

Chapter Twelve

In the narrow alley, the shot seemed to echo and reecho, and Sidney heard Carl make a strangled sound, like he wasn't expecting so much noise.

Sidney wasn't sure what her boss had intended, but the weapon was aimed low, and it looked like the bullet struck Luke in the leg, not in the central part of his body. Thank God.

Carl stared in horror as he realized that he'd actually shot a man.

Luke looked equally shocked as the leg crumpled under him and he sat down heavily in the alley.

Aghast, Sidney cried out as Luke leaned back against the wall, breathing hard, his face pale. She wanted to run to Luke, but Carl was still holding the gun.

"Oh Lord," she gasped. "Carl, are you crazy?"

He whipped around toward her, and she was sure she was going to get shot, too. "Shut up."

She clamped her lips together as he looked up and down the street to see if anybody had seen the impromptu drama.

Nobody shouted or came running, and Sidney cursed the early hour and the deserted downtown.

Carl turned again, advancing on Luke, who grimaced as he scooted backward on his bottom. But even the warrior wasn't going to get away from Carl with a bullet in his leg.

"Give me the box," the round little man snarled.

Sidney's heart raced as she tried to figure out what to do. As she looked wildly around, she saw a thick stick lying on the sidewalk. Snatching it up she moved in on Carl and poked the stick against his back.

"Drop the gun or I'll shoot," she said in a deadly calm voice.

He gasped and started to turn.

"Drop the gun," she ordered, "or I'll shoot you in the back, so help me God."

The gun clattered to the sidewalk.

"Kick it to Luke," she said, praying that Luke was in shape to grab it.

Carl kicked the gun across the pavement. It stopped a few feet from Luke, and he leaned over groaning as he picked it up and held it in a two-handed grip.

Now what, she thought. They'd disarmed Carl, but Luke was still wounded. He needed medical attention and they needed to figure out what to do with Carl.

She dropped the stick and walked toward Luke, making a big circle around the importer.

Kneeling down beside Luke, she looked at his pant leg. It was bloody but not sopping. Apparently the bullet hadn't hit an artery.

She spared her boss a scathing look. "You bastard."

He stood there, his lower lip trembling, probably realizing for the first time that he could have killed Luke.

While she was trying to figure out what to do, two SUV's pulled up at the entrance to the alley and two men jumped out. She sighed in relief when she saw Hunter Kelley and Jed Prentiss.

"Thank God," she breathed. "We're in bad trouble."

"What happened?" Hunter asked.

"My boss, Carl Peterbalm, shot Luke."

Jed swore. "Do you want to call the cops?"

She swallowed. "I—"

Luke interrupted before she could finish. "It's complicated. We can't call the police."

Hunter jerked his head toward Peterbalm. "What do we do with him?"

"If we leave him, there's no guarantee that he won't go to the cops and tell them we robbed him," Luke answered. "And no proof that he shot me, because I'm not going to be here."

"Then I guess we'd better take him with us," Hunter decided.

"Who the hell are you?" Carl demanded.

"The cavalry." Hunter took a step toward him.

Carl held up a hand as though he could push Hunter away. "Now wait a minute. Leave me alone!"

Hunter calmly slapped a cloth over Carl's face, and he went slack.

"What did you do to him?" Sidney gasped.

"Put him out. The anesthetic has an amnesiac effect."

"And now what?"

"We'll hold him until we can figure it out," Hunter answered.

"Is that legal?"

"No. But neither is shooting someone, or importing stolen goods," Hunter replied.

"You know about that?"

"Yeah. We've been investigating him." He turned toward Sidney. "And we made sure neither of you are involved with that." As he finished speaking, he climbed into the vehicle and drove away.

Apparently the Light Street crew had been prepared for a lot of different eventualities.

"Lucky we came out clean," Luke muttered.

"We had to be sure," Jed said as he bent down to tend to Luke. "By the way, I'm Jed Prentiss. I work for Randolph Security."

"Luke McMillan," he whispered.

"This is a hell of a way to meet. Um, want to give me the gun?"

Luke laughed. "Good idea." He let Jed lift the gun from his limp hand, click the safety and stuff it into his waistband.

"I'm going to cut your pant leg so I can see the wound," Jed said.

"Okay."

Jed looked at Sidney. "Keep watch."

She moved to the front of the alley while Jed ran back to the car and pulled a first aid kit from the floor of the backseat. Then he hurried to Luke again.

Sidney wanted to be at Luke's side, but she knew there wasn't anything constructive she could do. Instead she moved to the end of the alley and kept one eye on the street and one eye on the two men as Jed pulled out a penknife, opened it and cut away the bloody fabric. Perspiration had bloomed on Luke's forehead, and he groaned as Jed moved his leg.

"Sorry," the Light Street man muttered as he uncovered the injured area, which was in Luke's calf. Blood still oozed from a visible hole. "You need to see a doctor. I'm just an old battlefield medic."

"Okay."

Luke winced as Jed pressed gauze squares to the wound. "Sorry," he muttered again.

"Do what you have to," Luke answered.

Jed nodded and used a stretch bandage to hold the gauze in place. When he finished, he sat back on his heels. "Do you think you can you walk?"

"I hope so."

"Give me the box," Sidney said.

When he handed over the precious object without hesitation, her heart squeezed. He was showing his absolute trust in her.

"Thank you," she whispered as she cradled the box against her middle.

He gave her a small nod. Then Jed helped him up, and his face went white. She moved to Luke's other side, lending him more support him as he hobbled to the car.

When they reached the vehicle, she stood back while Jed eased Luke into the front seat, where he flopped down and sat with his head thrown back against the headrest.

"Where are you taking me?" Luke asked. "They'll ask questions about a gunshot wound."

"Don't worry. We have our people." Jed pulled away, his eyes meeting Sidney's in the rearview.

"Where is Hunter taking Carl Peterbalm?"

"To a safe place," Jed replied. Then he picked up a transmitter on the console and made a call. When someone at the other end of the line answered, he explained Luke's condition.

They drove through the downtown area and then into

the Latino neighborhood near Fells Point. Jed drove up to a three-story red brick structure that looked like it might have been a small, low-rise apartment building, only most of the windows were covered up. He turned in at a driveway that sloped down to wide garage door. It slid open, then closed behind him.

Overhead lights illuminated a garage area large enough to hold several dump trucks. As soon as the car stopped, a woman ran toward them, pushing a stretcher.

She and Jed helped Luke out of the car and onto the rolling bed, then toward an elevator directly in front of the car.

Sidney followed along as they traveled up two floors, then down a short corridor and into what looked like a hospital emergency room. They transferred Luke to an exam table, where a man in a white coat was waiting. While the nurse cut away the rest of Luke's jeans, the man spoke to him.

"I'm Doctor Miguel Valero. And this is Nurse Rosa Sanchez, who works at my clinic. We're going to take care of you."

Sidney had heard of the doctor. She knew he was active in the Latin American community, and Sabrina had told her he also worked for the Light Street Foundation. But she had no idea that this place existed.

Luke looked around. "If this isn't a hospital, what is it?"

"A facility maintained by the Light Street Foundation. We do community medicine here, but we also handle emergencies for the Light Street Detective Agency and their sister organization, Randolph Security."

Sidney took in the room. The equipment must have cost millions of dollars. And it was a secret.

"You have a bullet in your leg," Dr. Valero said to Luke. "I'm going to put you out while I remove it."

"No!" Luke sat up and tried to climb off the table.

The doctor and nurse pressed him back. "We have to remove the bullet," Dr. Valero said.

"I understand that," Luke acknowledged in a gritty voice. "But you cannot make me unconscious. I must keep an eye on the box."

Sidney hurried to his side and clasped his hand. "I'll hold it for you. You can trust me to do that."

He swung his head toward her. "I trust you, but I do not know these other people."

She wanted to point out how well they'd already handled this emergency, but she knew that logic wasn't going to work right now. Not when she was dealing with Zabastian's concerns, not Luke's.

She directed her next words to Dr. Valero. "He needs to stay awake. Can you give him something for the pain?"

"I can give him something, but if he's awake, it's going to hurt."

"Do it," Luke muttered.

The doctor looked resigned as he started an IV line in Luke's arm.

"Sidney must stay here with the box," Luke said.

"This isn't the operating room," the doctor said, his voice stern. "If she comes in there with us, she must put on a gown and mask."

Nodding to Luke, Sidney followed the doctor into a scrub room.

"I guess working with the Light Street group, you get some unusual cases," she said.

"Yes."

She cleared her throat. "Don't you have to report a gunshot wound?"

"In this facility, we have often bent the rules."

"Okay."

Apparently Valero wasn't going to say anymore, so she donned a gown and mask and waited for the doctor to scrub his hands and put on gloves. Then they both stepped into a small operating room.

Luke had his eyes fixed on the door. As soon as he saw her with the box, he seemed to relax.

She hurried to his side and reached for his hand, holding tight as the doctor walked to the other end of the table. A drape made it impossible for her to see what was happening, and she was grateful for that.

Seeing the pain on Luke's face as Valero worked was enough.

Luke stayed absolutely silent, but the way he gripped her hand told her that the procedure hurt.

It seemed to take centuries, but finally she heard the doctor make a satisfied sound. Coming around to Luke's other side, he held up the bullet in his gloved hand. "Here it is."

"Thank you," Sidney murmured, and Luke echoed the sentiment. His brow was covered with sweat, and his skin was gray, but the bullet was out.

"We have a special healing salve," Valero said, "courtesy of one of the Randolph Security men, Thorn Devereaux. He's been involved in various research projects for us."

"Okay," Luke said.

"You're lucky we have it."

He returned to the other end of the table and did something else that Sidney couldn't see. Then he pulled a sheet in place over the lower half of Luke's body.

They transferred him to a gurney again and wheeled him into the recovery room, and she stayed by his side, still clutching the box.

Finally, Luke was settled into a hospital bed. He lay still and pale against the pillow, with his eyes closed. When she sat down in the chair beside him, his eyes blinked open again and focused on her.

"How do you feel?" she asked.

"Not so bad. Thank you for staying with me."

"I'll do what you need me to do."

When she pressed her palm over his, he turned the hand over and knit his fingers with hers. "Help me stay awake."

"You shouldn't."

"Help me."

"Okay."

"Tell me about your life."

"What do you want to know?"

"I want to hear more about where you grew up," he whispered. "You said in Catonsville?"

"Yes. In an old house with a big yard. We didn't have a lot of money, but we had a lot of love. All the neighborhood kids were always at my house. Sometimes we'd have six or seven of them for lunch. Peanut butter and jelly sandwiches and canned soup."

"What did you play?" he murmured, and she wondered how long he could stay awake.

"We'd make forts on the porch, with a couple of sheets over two card tables. And in hot weather, we had a lemonade stand. And a wading pool in the backyard. We'd move it to a place in the yard where the ground had sunk in a little, so we'd have a deep spot in the pool."

"Um."

"And we'd squirt each other with the hose."

He made a barely audible sound. "What did you do in winter for fun?"

"My mom would bake cookies."

She thought Luke was going to sleep, but he asked, "What kind?"

"Chocolate chip and molasses were my favorite."

"You don't like oatmeal raisin?"

"They're good too."

She wanted to ask questions about his childhood, but she knew he was in no shape to keep up his end of the conversation.

He murmured, "Christmas?"

"We'd go out in the country and cut down our own tree. And it was always so big we had to move the furniture around the living room. Then Dad would get the decorations from the attic. We made a lot of them ourselves."

"It sounds like a good family time."

"Yes."

"And what do you want for the future?" he whispered, his voice barely above a whisper.

She went rigid. Was he asking about them, or the personal plans she'd made? And how much did she dare to say?

"I want to be like you," she said.

"Huh?"

"I want my own business. I want to be my own boss. I'd do that if I could afford it."

"What…kind of business?"

"Antiques. I know the field. That's one of the reasons Carl Peterbalm hired me."

"And he wants…to get into your pants," Luke muttered. Apparently the medicine had undermined his ability to censor his speech.

She laughed. "Yes, but he didn't even get close." Without elaborating, she went back to her own plans. "But I'd need a shop and also inventory."

She got caught up in talking about what she'd been dreaming of for years, until Luke made a sharp noise, and her gaze flew to him. Then she saw he was snoring.

"So much for fascinating you with my daydreams," she said in a low voice, then looked up to see Dr. Valero in the doorway.

"He wanted to stay awake," she whispered.

"He needs to sleep." The doctor gave her a considering look. "And so do you."

She looked from the doctor to Luke. "What did you give him?" she asked.

"A minimal dose of painkiller. To help him rest so his body can heal."

He'd told her to rest too. But she said, "I promised to guard the box."

"You can keep it with you. Nobody's getting into the building to steal it."

She sighed. "I understand. But Luke doesn't know you." Not to mention Zabastian, she thought.

"We'll pull a bed up beside his. You can sleep there."

"Thanks."

Sidney gently untangled her hand from Luke's. She intended to stay awake. But as soon as she slipped off her shoes and lay down on the bed the staff brought in, fatigue washed over her and the world faded. She awoke with a start, disoriented and frightened.

Her head swung to the side, and she saw that Luke had made a strangled sound as he woke suddenly.

"It's okay. I'm here," she said as she scrambled off her bed and leaned over him.

"The box?"

"Right here." She picked it up from the bedside table and showed it to him. "I said you could trust these people."

He sighed and settled back in the bed. His face was haggard and unshaven, but he looked like he was feeling better.

Moments later, the door opened, and Dr. Valero came in.

"How long was I asleep?" Luke asked.

"Eight hours."

He sucked in a sharp breath. "Too long."

"You needed to heal. Twice that long would have been better."

Despite Luke's protests, the doctor asked, "How are you feeling?"

Luke took a breath as he considered the question. When he flexed his leg, he looked shocked. "It's…not so bad."

"I told you we had a salve with extraordinary healing properties."

"I wasn't in shape to focus on that," Luke muttered.

After the doctor cranked up his bed, Luke inspected the room. "Is there a bathroom anywhere around?"

"Yes." Dr. Valero pointed to a door at the side of the room. "Right over there."

He and Nurse Sanchez helped Luke ease off the bed. Sidney held her breath as she watched him stand with the help of a cane the doctor had provided.

Luke was still shaky, but she was shocked when she saw him put weight on the leg. Giving her a look of triumph, he started toward the bathroom.

While he was gone, Sidney went out into the hall and found her friend Sabrina sitting on a comfortable sofa.

Sabrina jumped up. "How are you?"

"Better. And so is Luke." She kept her gaze steady as she cleared her throat. "So Light Street knew about Carl's illegal activities?"

"They've been investigating him for several months."

"And me?"

"I told them you couldn't be involved," Sabrina assured her.

Sidney swallowed. "Thanks. But I gather they confirmed that on their own. And also investigated Luke."

"Yes. But don't hold it against them. They were doing their job."

"I understand."

"How is Luke?" Sabrina asked, changing the subject.

"He's recovering."

"And the warrior is still with him?"

"So you believed that part."

"Yes I did. And so did Dan."

Sidney breathed out a little sigh. "Did you, uh, tell anyone else about the warrior?"

"Not yet."

"I'm not looking forward to it."

"We'll do it in a while. You probably want to use the bathroom and take a shower."

"Do I look like I need it?"

"Yes."

"What about the box?"

"I'll keep it safe. Go on. It's all right."

Sidney considered the offer. She trusted Sabrina and everybody in this building. But she knew Luke was still not sure about her friends.

"I'll take good care of it," Sabrina said, then cleared her throat. "There's something I'd better tell you."

"Something bad?"

"I'm sorry. But the guys who were after you broke into your apartment and trashed it."

Sidney groaned.

"We've had a crew putting it back together."

"You didn't have to do that."

"We didn't want you to come home to that."

Sidney nodded. "I can't thank you enough for everything you've done."

"That's what friends are for."

Sidney handed over the box. Sabrina made an appreciative sound as she took it in her hands and turned it.

"It's very old."

"I know."

"Go take your shower." She pointed to a ladies' room down the hall. "There's a change of clothing there."

Sidney went away. The "ladies' room" was actually built like a luxury bathroom in a private residence with a marble counter, an enormous shower, and a separate soaking tub. Not only was there a variety of toilet articles, she also saw several changes of clothing in the walk-in closet. She would have liked to pamper herself, but she allowed herself only a minimal amount of time to make herself presentable.

When she stepped into the hall again, dressed in slacks and a comfortable knit top, she had a moment of panic when she found Sabrina missing. But she followed the sound of voices to a comfortable lounge where Luke was lying on a hospital bed, dressed in a T-shirt and sweatpants. The box was on the table beside him, and his hands were wrapped around a mug.

He looked up with a feeling of relief when he spotted her.

"I'm sorry I was gone so long," she said. "What are you drinking?"

"Chicken soup," the doctor explained. "It's part of the healing process," he added with a grin.

Other people in the room were also eating—sandwiches and salads from a table along the wall.

Sidney's stomach rumbled, and she flushed.

"Help yourself," Jed said.

"Thanks." She looked around the room. Hunter was there. Also Sabrina and her husband, Dan Cassidy. As well as Nick Vickers. She'd met all the people except Rosa Sanchez at parties that Sabrina had given.

"Did you meet everyone?" she asked Luke.

"Yes, while you were gone."

Sidney helped herself to some chicken salad and looked at the crowd. These people had broken the law to help her and Luke with no questions asked. Now they were waiting to find out how Sidney and Luke had ended up here, but she was still nervous about telling her story. So she asked Hunter, "Where's Carl Peterbalm?"

"In another part of this building, sleeping comfortably."

The group had left a chair beside the bed, and she sat

down next to Luke. When she was seated, Jed cleared his throat. "So are you going to tell us what this is all about?"

Luke shifted uncomfortably on the bed.

"I think we'd better get it over with," she murmured.

Luke gave her a long look. "You mean you want me to tell them that I'm not just Luke McMillan. That inside me is the spirit of an ancient warrior named Zabastian who was locked in the box?"

Chapter Thirteen

Sidney wasn't surprised to hear exclamations and in-drawn breaths around the room.

She watched all eyes turn to Luke and saw his defiant expression.

Feeling her stomach knot, she looked at Sabrina. "What now?" she mouthed.

Her friend didn't answer, but she looked hopefully toward the doorway.

After a moment of silence, Sidney's only option was a reply to Luke. "Yeah, that."

She'd hoped Sabrina could help. But it looked like she and Luke were on their own. Speaking quickly, she began to explain what had happened.

"I know that sounds crazy. I had trouble believing it at first. But I've spent enough time with Luke to know it's true." She recounted the events at the warehouse when Luke opened the box. "The warrior was put inside the box a long time ago to protect it," she concluded.

"The box is ancient," Sabrina added. "I can vouch for that."

"How ancient?" a voice said from the doorway, and

Sidney looked up to see another one of the Randolph men, Thorn Devereaux, standing there. Mostly he worked in the lab, but apparently he'd come down here for this meeting. He was tall and dark, and his dark eyes were fixed on Luke.

"The Moon Priests constructed the box more than two thousand years ago," Luke said, his voice defying anyone to challenge him.

Thorn tipped his head to the side, studying Luke for long moments.

"Sabrina called and told me."

Sidney gave her friend an inquiring look.

Sabrina shrugged, and Sidney looked back at Thorn again. His thoughts seemed to be turned inward. After a few moments, he said something in a language she couldn't understand. At first he sounded like he was picking his way through the vocabulary and sentence structure, but as he spoke, his voice became more confident.

Luke looked astonished, then happy. As soon as Thorn stopped talking, he answered immediately in what sounded like the same language.

The two men spoke rapidly back and forth, their dialogue completely private, because nobody else was equipped to understood.

Thorn said something else to Luke, and Sidney was pretty sure it translated to "Let me handle it."

Turning to the group, he said, "He's telling the truth. He's speaking in an ancient language from the Indian subcontinent. Even if he could read it, there's not a chance in hell that anybody but a native speaker would know how to pronounce it today."

"Or you," Sabrina said, shooting Sidney a triumphant look. "Because you were there."

Sidney goggled at her. "What do you mean he was there? He's a time traveler?"

"Sort of. We don't usually talk about it, but Thorn was part of an expedition that was sent here—to our planet— by another civilization more than fifteen hundred years ago. He was their exobiologist and their language expert. He went out of his way to get to know the people they met. When he protested the way some of the members of the expedition were treating the natives, they put him in suspended animation and left him here before they took off for home."

Jed entered the conversation. "He was rescued by Cassie Devereaux, my wife's sister. Otherwise, he would have died. He married Cassie and took her name."

"So you…you were alive when Zabastian was living?" Sidney clarified.

"Yes, and I know about the Temple of the Moon. We studied the religion. They were very advanced for their time. They were monotheists. They also believed they had a sacred mission from God to keep mankind on the right path."

Luke cut in swiftly. "They didn't just *believe* it; it's true. The box was stolen a few months ago, and it arrived here in a shipment of stolen antiques. I must return it to the Master of the Moon as soon as possible."

All over the room, people began talking to each other, creating a babble of sound. Then Luke's voice boomed out. Only it wasn't exactly Luke. Sidney knew that Zabastian was speaking. "I do not have time to waste. I must get to the Moon Temple."

"Where is it?"

"I do not know! I was about to find out when the Poisoned Ones broke into our hiding place." He looked around the room. "Do you have a computer nearby where I can get e-mail?"

"An ancient warrior getting e-mail?" Jed asked.

"We use what is available. Luke knows how to use the computer very well."

"You can use my desktop," Dr. Valero said. "The connection is secure."

Luke pushed himself off the bed, and Sidney watched him carefully.

"It's better if you use the cane for the time being," the doctor said.

Luke scowled, but he took the cane, leaning on it as he followed the doctor out of the room. When Sidney got up, he shook his head.

"You stay here and answer their questions."

"Is that an order?" she asked.

Instead of giving a snap answer, he considered the question carefully.

SMITH, JONES AND BROWN CRUISED slowly down a residential street in their rental car. They had hidden in the attic of the house, hoping they wouldn't have to shoot their way out.

Apparently the police had been convinced that the only fugitives were the man and the woman so they'd left very quickly.

The trio emerged when the coast was clear.

After their recent confrontation, they were somewhat the worse for wear. Any other men would have been in the hospital. But they had the stamina—or the desperation—to keep going.

Unfortunately, they had lost Peterbalm. Now they were considering what to do.

Brown looked around as though he expected an angel of the Lord to descend from the heavens and smite them. In fact, that was a lot like what he was thinking. Although the terms were different, he knew they were in serious trouble.

"If we can't find McMillan and the woman, we have to find the temple and intercept them," Smith said.

"That's dangerous," Jones objected.

Smith shrugged. "It may be our last shot at the box."

"How do we find the temple?" Brown asked.

Smith pointed to the backseat. "We have the computer. We can duplicate McMillan's search."

"You can do that?" Brown asked.

"I have computer experience," he said, and Brown heaved a sigh. So much for certainty. Still, it was their only option, barring driving around the city looking for the man and woman.

"They had help getting away," Jones said.

"You're sure of that?" Brown challenged.

"Somebody's hiding them," Smith said.

"Peterbalm switched sides?" Brown asked.

"We can't exactly ask him," Smith snapped. He looked back at the computer again. "I need a place where I can work on this machine."

"Where?"

"A hotel room," he said. "Someplace close so we can get there quickly when I find the location of the temple."

SIDNEY HEARD LUKE SOFTEN HIS voice, as if remembering that men didn't give women orders in today's world, unless they were paying for the privilege, like Carl Peterbalm.

"Please stay here and tell them what happened to us."

She felt her chest go tight. She wanted to stay with him, but she understood the advantage of their each taking on a different task.

"Okay."

As he limped down the hall, leaning on the cane, she began speaking again, telling the Light Street people about the three men, the shoot-out in the garage, and the rest of it. She ended with the story of Carl Peterbalm shooting Luke, and Hunter and Jed showing up just in time.

"You've had quite an exciting time," Thorn said when she had finished.

"Unfortunately."

"So now what?" Hunter asked.

"I give the box back," Luke said from the doorway.

"You got a message from the Master of the Moon?" she asked.

"Yes."

"You should have told him you're not well enough to go to the temple yet," she objected.

"I'm mending very quickly, thanks to…" He stopped and looked at Thorn. "Did the salve come from your people?"

"Yes. With the limited resources on your world, we can only make it in small quantities."

Luke flexed his leg. "Thank you for letting me have some. I need to be steady on my feet when I go to the temple."

Sidney narrowed her eyes as she watched him. No matter what happened after they returned the box, she wasn't going to leave him on his own now. "You're not going by yourself," she said.

"I have to."

She swept her hand around the room. "We've got all these people trained in covert operations who can make sure you get there safely."

"But the temple is in the city. And they'd call attention to me," Luke said. "I must do it alone."

"No. I'm going with you." As she spoke, she scrambled desperately for a good reason and came up with a logical rationale. "You need someone, in case you get into trouble. And I've earned the right to be that person," she said, then held her breath, waiting for his answer.

"All right," he finally said.

"You shouldn't be going at all," Dr. Valero interjected, addressing himself to Luke.

Sidney gave him a grateful look, but Luke only shook his head. "I have to."

"Give yourself a few hours. If you're trying to stay inconspicuous, it makes sense to wait until after dark."

Luke considered the advice.

When he nodded, Sidney breathed out a small sigh.

"You can send a message to the Master of the Moon telling him that you have been shot trying to keep the box safe. I'm sure he will take that into consideration."

Luke agreed.

She felt her heart leap. If they stayed here for the rest of the day, that would give her more time to spend with Luke before they left.

But the doctor's next words dashed that hope. "You

should sleep as much as possible. I can give you something that will put you out for a few hours."

"The box…"

"You know it will be safe here," Thorn said. "I will keep it for you, so Sidney can also get some rest."

"Thank you," she breathed.

She waited until the doctor had taken Luke to a bedroom down the hall. Then she let Rosa Sanchez show her to another room—with a promise that she'd wake her up as soon as Luke was awake again.

Did she trust him not to leave her here?

Her chest tightened when she considered that question. But she really had no option. She knew Zabastian was making the decisions. He was a stubborn man, and she couldn't dictate terms to him. Too bad he couldn't simply disappear. He'd almost gotten her and Luke killed. And he might well do it again.

Now all she could do was pray that they made it through the completion of the mission.

As she pulled off her clothes and lay down, she thought about the man down the hall.

She'd said she wanted Zabastian to go away. But that wasn't entirely true. In some ways, Zabastian had changed Luke for the better. The question was—who would he be when Zabastian left him?

What would happen between her and Luke then? Did they have any kind of future together? She knew there was absolutely no way to figure that out until after he returned the box.

DOWN THE HALL, LUKE STOOD beside the bed, feeling tugging at him. The doctor had given him a pill to take, and he'd said he would. But he didn't need it. Zabastian could use his meditation techniques to induce sleep, if that's what they decided.

You're a chicken, the warrior said inside his skull.

About what? he asked, even when he knew exactly what Zabastian was talking about.

You could have taken her to bed with you.

And made love with a bullet wound in my leg?

You could have lain on your back and enjoyed her attentions. She would have been glad to accommodate you.

The warrior suddenly filled his head with some very vivid and very erotic pictures. Luke felt his body instantly respond.

I guess you're recovering nicely from the gunshot.

Shut up, Luke growled. *Are you still thinking that you can control women in this century?*

I wasn't suggesting control. I was thinking about cooperation.

And then what? Luke challenged. *Are you pretending that I have a future with her?*

To his gratification, the warrior was silent.

Everything's going to change in a few hours. I have no idea who Luke McMillan is going to be when you complete your assignment and leave.

Are you afraid of proceeding on your own? the warrior instantly asked.

I'm not going to answer that, Luke shot back, for all the good the denial did him. He knew that Zabastian could read him as easily as he'd read that strange language on the computer screen.

I apologize for interrupting your life, the warrior suddenly said.

Luke was astonished by the silent words and by his own answer.

My life wasn't going so well before that.

Of course it was. You didn't have the formal education most people would think you needed to succeed in this society. But you did very well, anyway.

So I made money. That didn't get me what I wanted.

Cutting right to the heart of the matter, Zabastian said, *Sidney is impressed with your business skills.*

Luke sighed. *I don't want to talk about Sidney.*

Okay. We should sleep while we have the chance. Then we can return the box.

And there's still a chance that both of us can end up dead? Luke clarified.

Let us be optimistic, the warrior answered. Luke caught something lurking at the edge of Zabastian's thoughts. He wanted to get some clarification, but before he could continue the conversation, he felt his brain and body go into shutdown mode.

He tried to shout a protest, but he didn't get the chance.

A KNOCK ON THE DOOR WOKE Sidney. She looked at the clock on the bedside table and realized she'd slept for another seven hours.

"Come in," she called out.

Sabrina opened the door, carrying a tray with a mug of something.

"Thorn's power formula," Sabrina said when Sidney took a cautious sip.

"It's not too bad."

"You need energy, and it's the fastest way to get it."

The other woman was also holding a dark plastic garment bag.

"Luke asked you to wear this," she said, discarding the covering. Inside was a dress that looked like something she might have worn to church on Easter Sunday. It was blue silk with a matching jacket. Delicate underwear, pantyhose and high-heeled shoes were also included in a separate bag.

"Kind of fancy," she murmured.

"I guess the Temple of the Moon is kind of fancy," Sabrina answered.

"Have you ever heard of it?" Sidney asked.

"No. But Luke made it sound like the location was hidden."

"Right. He didn't even know where it was until he got that last e-mail."

Sabrina glanced at the clock. "I should go and let you get dressed."

Sidney stepped into the bathroom, then took off the T-shirt she'd worn to bed and dressed in the fancy outfit. It fit perfectly, and she even found some cosmetics in the bathroom that she used to make up her face.

She felt like she was getting ready for a very special event—which was true. She just wished she'd had some advanced warning about what was going to happen. Still, she couldn't help a disturbing thought from skittering through her mind. Luke was going to need her.

She felt that even more keenly when she picked up the small purse that came with the outfit. It felt strangely heavy. When she looked inside, she found a snub-nosed revolver and a cell phone.

Sidney's heart started pounding as she took in the special equipment.

When she stepped into the hall, Luke was standing a few yards away.

Her breath caught when she looked at him. He'd carefully combed his hair and he'd dressed in a dark suit. Instead of gripping the cane, he now carried a soft-sided briefcase which she assumed held the box. The box—and probably the same kind of equipment she'd been given, in case they got into trouble.

She resolutely put the danger out of her mind and focused on Luke.

"You look fantastic," she said, seeing he was taking her in with the same admiration.

The look in his eye made her heart leap.

"So do you," he murmured.

Like we're going to a wedding, she thought, then was glad she hadn't voiced the observation aloud. That would have embarrassed both of them.

Hunter came down the hall. He too had changed into dark slacks and a blue shirt.

"There's been a development," he said stiffly.

"What?"

"The cops have gone into high gear looking for you. Someone reported the shoot-out with Peterbalm. Only they don't seem to get it that you weren't doing any shooting."

"Damn," Sidney muttered.

"You're wanted for questioning."

Luke glanced at Sidney. "You can stay here where it's safe."

"I could. But I'm not," she said. "Anyway, if they think

we're on the run, they won't expect us to be dressed like this."

Luke nodded, then turned to Hunter. "Let's go."

Dr. Valero was waiting by the elevator as were most of the people who had heard their strange story.

"I want to thank you for everything," Luke said stiffly.

"We were glad to help out," Sabrina said, then added, "Let us know what happens."

Sidney gave a quick nod. She was waiting to find that out herself.

They took the elevator to the garage, where Hunter ushered them to a Ford SUV.

She and Luke both climbed into the backseat and buckled up so that they were sitting at opposite sides of the vehicle. She wanted to slide over and sit next to Luke, but she felt frozen in place.

"Where to?" Hunter asked.

Luke gave him two cross streets.

Sidney looked at him in surprise. "There's a temple around there?"

"That's the location they gave me."

"It's in your old neighborhood, right?"

"Yeah."

She tried to picture the streets. They were in a residential neighborhood, a typical Baltimore setting with row houses lining the sidewalks. She'd been there many times because some of the city's best ethnic restaurants were located nearby, but she had never noticed anything like a Temple of the Moon.

Hunter drove to the corner Luke had mentioned and pulled up at the curb.

"You're sure you want me to drop you off?" he asked.

"Yes," Luke answered. "And don't hang around."

Hunter looked like he thought they were making a mistake, but he only said, "Good luck."

Luke glanced up and down the street, then toward Sidney. "You can stay here if you want," he offered one more time.

"Stop trying to get rid of me." She wanted to tell him she thought he was going to need her, but she knew he wouldn't like hearing that assessment.

Silently, they both got out and stood on the corner. Luke looked like he was trying to figure out where they were going. When he started down the block and then stopped, she wanted to ask him if he'd gotten the address wrong.

But just then she spotted a police car. It was cruising slowly down the street, headed straight for them.

Luke cursed under his breath, his hand dipping inside the briefcase.

Sidney's pulse had already started pounding. It pounded even harder as she watched Luke's hand disappear into the bag. "If you're going for a gun, stop!" she hissed. "You can't shoot the cops."

"You're right," he conceded, easing his fingers back out of the bag. Instead, he grabbed her hand and hustled her back the way they'd come.

But the cop had apparently spotted them, fancy outfits and all.

Luke ushered her around the corner, then into a small grocery store.

The man behind the counter looked up. "May I help you?" He gave them a second look. "Luke McMillan? All dressed up like you got a bonus from the mob."

"It's me. But I'm not working for the mob. And we're just passing through," Luke said as he led Sidney to the back of the shop.

"I thought you'd gotten your life on the right track. Are you in trouble again?" the man called out.

"This time it's a frame-up, Mr. Donetti. If the cops ask, tell them you haven't seen me."

He hustled Sidney into a storeroom, then out the back of the shop and down the alley, where he pressed her into the shadow of a storage shed. When footsteps came running up the alley, he reached for the door handle, but it was held closed by a lock and hasp. As she watched, Luke reached for the lock and closed his fist around it. She saw his intense focus as he gave the mechanism a long slow twist. Sidney had seen enough of the warrior's power that she wasn't even surprised when the hasp snapped off. Removing it from the door, he slipped the lock into his pocket, then eased the door open and ushered her inside.

The alley had been dark. The interior of the shed was almost pitch-black.

As they stood in the darkness hearing heavy footsteps coming toward them, Sidney felt her heart blocking her windpipe. But Luke put down the briefcase again and reached around her so that he could grab the door handle and hold it closed.

The footsteps came to the shed and stopped. Then they continued on, and she breathed out a small sigh. But her relief had come too quickly. Moments later, she heard someone else approaching, someone who also stopped in front of the shed.

A large fist banged on the door and she had to clench

her teeth to keep from making a sound. When the banging didn't open the door, she felt someone try to pull it open. But Luke must have kept his grip on the inside handle, and the barrier remained closed.

The man on the other side made a rough sound then gave a sharp yank, but Luke was the stronger of the two, and he was able to maintain the integrity of their hiding place.

Finally, after another sound of frustration from the outside of the shed, the footsteps receded.

In the darkness, Luke cupped his hand around Sidney's head and pressed her face against his shoulder. With his mouth against her ear, he whispered, "Don't move."

Her pulse still pounding, she silently nodded against his cheek. She and Luke stood together in the dark, and she clung to him for strength and comfort. When his other arm came up to cradle her against his body, she melted into him, grateful for the contact. She was very conscious that this was the first time he'd held her since the cave, and it was wonderful to be back in his arms, even under these circumstances.

Maybe this was the last time he would ever hold her. She ached to press her lips to his, to taste him. And, more than that, to know how he really felt about her.

After Dr. Valero had taken the bullet out, she'd stayed with Luke, and he'd asked her to talk to him. She'd been glad to do it. More than glad, she'd been elated that he'd turned to her. But their relationship hadn't been the same since then. She was sure he'd deliberately put distance between them.

She wanted to know why. Because he thought there was no future for them? Because he knew that something bad was going to happen?

A kiss might have told her where they stood with each other. But she knew she dared not distract him that much. He was trying to keep them safe.

From the police? The Poisoned Ones?

They'd hurt those men, but she had no reason to believe they hadn't gotten away. If Luke could find the Temple of the Moon, maybe they could do the same thing, and maybe they'd spotted her and Luke.

She sighed and moved her head, then stroked her hand across his broad back, loving the solid feel of his muscles.

"Luke?"

He stiffened. "Don't."

"Don't what?"

"Don't start anything with me."

She felt a terrible hollow place open up inside her. He had as much as told her it was all over.

Well, what had she thought would happen? That he'd ask her to marry him when the cops and the bad guys stopped chasing them?

She heard him make a sound deep in his chest, and her heart leaped. He was going to say something about them!

But the words that came out of his mouth were all business. "I think we can make a run for the temple."

"What temple?"

"You didn't see it?"

"No."

He made a frustrated sound. "It's right between number 57 and 59. Right up the block from where Hunter let us off."

She moved back, lifting her face toward his, wishing

she could see his expression in the dark. "Luke, what are you trying to pull? There's nothing between 57 and 59. They're row houses—right next to each other."

Chapter Fourteen

In the darkness, Luke struggled to control a spurt of fear. If Sidney couldn't get into the temple, then she would be outside alone and unprotected.

Damn, he should have made her stay with her friends. But he'd wanted to keep her with him as long as possible, and he had to protect her.

"You can't see the building?" he asked. "Between numbers 57 and 59," he repeated, in case she was looking in the wrong place. "The house with the blue woodwork and the one with the yellow door."

She answered in a small voice, her one word tearing at him like the claws of a bird of prey.

"No."

Fighting to keep his wildly swinging emotions under control, he scraped around in his mind, trying to help her figure out how to bring the temple into her vision. It was so natural to him, now that he'd absorbed the warrior's essence. And he'd assumed it would be the same for her.

Finally, he came up with an analogy. "Have you ever looked at any of those Magic Eye books and seen a flat picture change to three-dimensional?"

"Yes. But what does that have to do with it?"

"So you know you have to change the way you look at the page. It's kind of like crossing your eyes."

"Yes."

"It's the same for the Moon Temple. If you stare at the line between those two houses and change your vision, you'll see the doorway of the temple. And the rest of the building is in back of it."

"What if I can't see it?"

He tried to sound confident. "If you can't see it, just run for the doorway, and the priests will let you in."

Together, Luke and Zabastian prayed that it was true. Prayed with every fiber of belief that he'd ever possessed. Because if it wasn't, they were both in big trouble.

Sidney must have caught the hesitation in his voice. She put her hands on his shoulders, gripping him through the suit coat.

He heard her swallow hard. "You mean, you might get inside, and I can't?"

He felt a kind of desperation rise inside him. "That might be true. I don't know. We just have to have faith."

"Faith in moon priests?"

"Yes."

"A cult that died out a thousand years ago?"

Frustration made his words choppy. "I told you, they didn't die out. They just went into hiding."

"Okay."

He changed the subject abruptly. "We can't stay in this shed."

"Who do you think was out there?"

"The police. The Poisoned Ones," he answered, hoping the reality would jolt her into action. "We have to make a run for the temple and hope we can get inside before anybody grabs us. If you can't see the door, follow me."

She dragged in a breath and let it out. "Okay."

He reached inside the briefcase and pulled out the shoulder strap, which he attached in the dark. When he was sure it was secure, he slung it over his head and across his chest so that the bag hung against his back, leaving his hands free.

Then he eased the door open and peered into the alley. As far as he could see, it was clear. But he knew someone could be waiting in the shadows for them to make a move.

He had no idea how the Poisoned Ones would have figured out where to find the temple, but he couldn't shake the feeling that they were around here somewhere waiting. He didn't tell any of that to Sidney as he led her down the alley.

His leg was starting to throb, but he ignored the pain. He'd just been shot the day before, and under ordinary circumstances he wouldn't have been able to walk without crutches. Now he gritted his teeth and kept going, telling himself that he only had a few more minutes before he reached safety.

At the entrance to the street, he stopped again and slung his arm around Sidney's shoulder, then bent to whisper in her ear. "Do you see the houses?"

"Yes."

"Look at the line between them."

"I am!"

"And you don't see anything?"

"No."

He repressed a curse, silently admitting that if she couldn't see it, she might be barred from entering. But maybe he could get her inside, or maybe the priests would take pity on them.

A rough sound rose in his throat. The priests had never taken pity on the warrior. They had insured his loyalty, then doomed him to hell for centuries.

"What?" Sidney whispered.

"Nothing. Follow me." He stepped out of the alley and hurried to the corner, hearing her high-heeled shoes clicking right behind him.

Damn. That was another mistake he'd made. He should have told her to wear something more practical, but he'd wanted to see her all dressed up.

They crossed the street, and he stopped for a moment, fighting the tension in his gut.

"Do you see it yet?"

"I'm trying."

His mouth dry as sand, he started across the street. At that moment, a shape flew out of the darkness, heading directly for him. Not one shape. Three.

The Poisoned Ones. Desperate to get the box before it was too late.

Sidney screamed. As Luke whirled, facing the first attacker, he knew he had to relinquish command of his body again.

This time, he asked Zabastian to take over, feeling the man's martial arts training seize his muscles and tendons.

From the corner of his eye, he saw Sidney stand paralyzed for a long moment. Then she reached into the small purse she still carried.

He'd forgotten about the purse. Forgotten that Hunter had told him she would be armed.

"Run for the temple," he shouted.

She didn't reply, and she didn't run.

Instead she pivoted, facing one of the men as he charged toward Luke.

He still saw her only from the corner of his vision as he flung one of the Poisoned Ones to the ground, then blocked a lethal blow from one of the others.

As he whirled again, the bad leg buckled, and he had to call on every ounce of discipline he possessed to keep from falling over.

A shot rang out, and he realized that Sidney had fired her gun. One of the bad guys staggered but kept coming.

"Kill the woman," he shouted.

Another one of them switched his attention from Luke to Sidney, lunging at her.

Luke threw out his arm, catching the man in the neck and sending him sprawling in the street.

At least no cars were coming, Luke thought with one corner of his mind. Then he heard a siren in the distance and he knew that they had only a few moments to get to safety.

"Run for the temple," he shouted to Sidney,

She stayed beside him, firing again as one of the bad guys got up and charged one more time.

He stopped the man with a kick, then grabbed Sidney's shoulder and urged her toward the temple.

With the assailants right behind them, they staggered together across the street toward the spot where he knew they could find safety.

As they drew nearer, Sidney gasped. "I see it."

"Thank God. Get inside."

One of the Poisoned Ones had given up. The other two put on a burst of speed, desperate to win the prize they had come here to steal.

One of them made a grab for the briefcase, but Sidney brought the gun down on his hand.

He grunted, but he didn't stop running.

When he grabbed her by the hair, she screamed. Luke turned and chopped down with his hand on the man's fingers. He let go, and she stumbled along, freed from the attacker's grip.

Police cars rounded the corner with lights flashing as Luke grabbed Sidney's arm and pulled her up the temple steps to the stone archway carved with the phases of the moon.

Below the arch were huge wooden doors, banded with iron. They could never have fit in the space between the two row houses. Not in real life. But he had always known the doors would be here when he found the temple, even if he couldn't explain how they existed in time and space.

They loomed in front of him, overshadowing the two buildings that were nominally on either side.

Sidney reached the door and grasped the handle, trying to pull it open, but nothing happened, and Luke felt a terrible pressure inside his chest.

Even if you could see the doors, they didn't open for everyone. As he raised his hand to pound, the opposite door creaked on its huge hinges. With a prayer of thanks, he pushed Sidney inside, then followed behind her.

Stumbling, she tried to catch herself but ended up sprawling ignominiously on the inlaid tile floor. She was lying at the feet of a man wearing sandals and rich blue robes.

Zabastian remembered Father Delanos from the last time he had defended the Master's property. His hair was gray, but his face was smooth. Really he didn't look like he'd been living for over five hundred years.

Sidney was gasping for breath. Zabastian was struggling to maintain some semblance of dignity, but it was difficult when they'd come flying through the doors like refugees from a tornado.

Beside him, Sidney sat up and looked around in awe at the rich murals on the walls. They showed the night sky, with the moon at the center of each picture. Each was bordered by gold tiles inlaid into the stone.

"It's real," she gasped.

"Of course it's real," the Grand Master said.

She climbed shakily to her feet and stood swaying on unsteady legs. "But how? I mean, I've never heard of you."

"We decided centuries ago that we did not want to set ourselves up as a rival to the world's great religions, so we have gone underground."

"Okay, I get that part. But that doesn't explain this building being here where I've never seen it before. And nobody else can see it, either. How is it possible?"

The Grand Master spoke with infinite patience. "Because we can bend the fabric of the space-time continuum."

"Then why did you need Luke to bring you the box?" she asked, cutting to the heart of the matter.

"We have great power inside this building. Once we leave, we are at a considerable disadvantage."

Luke answered the question. "He'll die if he leaves."

"Why?"

"I should introduce myself," the man said. "I am Father Delanos. And I am very old. Older than I look. Inside this building, time stands almost still, and I age very slowly."

Sidney gasped as she took that in. Tipping her head to the side, she looked at the priest with new eyes.

"If someone else told me that, I'd think…." Her voice trailed off. "But I believe you."

Father Delanos acknowledged the words with a little smile.

Sidney cleared her throat. "Thank you for letting me in. Why did you change your mind?"

He smiled again. "Because you were fighting to save the life of Zabastian. We couldn't leave you outside to face the Poisoned Ones or your police."

"Thank you."

"And thank you, as well. You are a very brave woman."

"I didn't feel brave. I felt scared."

"Fear is often the spur to bravery," Father Delanos said. He gestured to Sidney. "I want to welcome you properly. Come in."

He led the two of them down a long hallway, and Luke saw Sidney still looking around as though she couldn't believe the reality of the temple.

"This place is big," she murmured. "But it takes up no space on the outside."

"One of our little tricks," the high priest said as he ushered them into a small sitting room.

It was furnished with low couches and rich Oriental

rugs with moon and star designs woven into the pattern. A tray sat on a carved wooden table.

"Sit down and be comfortable."

Luke pulled the briefcase off of his back and handed it to Father Delanos. "The box is in here."

"Yes. Thank you. We will deal with it soon. Sit down," he said again.

You've been struggling to get the box here, and he's not acting like it's important, Luke silently commented.

He will get to it in good time.

They sat, and Father Delanos poured a drink from a crystal bottle into a golden cup and handed it to Sidney. She sniffed the contents, then looked at the priest.

"I hope this isn't like that box of chocolates in Narnia, where Edwin ate one and it enslaved him to the White Witch."

The priest laughed. "No. Of course not."

Luke felt his stomach tighten. "It's a potion that will lengthen your life," he said.

Her eyes widened, and she looked at the priest again. "Why are you giving it to me?"

"As a reward," Father Delanos said.

She eyed him and then Luke. "But it was a punishment for Zabastian, wasn't it?"

The priest nodded. "Rewards and punishments depend on the circumstances."

She took a cautious sip, looking like she expected it to taste like medicine. "It's good."

Luke drank, too. Whether reward or punishment, he would find out soon enough.

He felt Zabastian quietly waiting as he drained the small cup. More than ever, he was sure the warrior was hiding something, and he'd like to know what it was. But Zabastian made no comment.

"It is time," the Master said.

Luke stood.

When Sidney stayed on the couch, the old man said, "You have earned the right to come with us."

"Thank you."

"Carry the briefcase," Father Delanos said to Luke.

He picked up the case with the box and the priest led them out of the room and to the back of the building. They stepped into a small chapel with rows of wooden pews and fine Oriental rugs covering the stone floor. Although it was night outside in the city, light filtered in through windows that were set high above eye level.

Zabastian had always wondered what the view would be if you could climb up and see out. Maybe just blue sky. Maybe the moon shining in a daylight sky.

Men in brightly colored robes sat in the pews, making the room into a rainbow of color. Some wore yellow, others red or green or blue, and Zabastian silently explained that the robes denoted their status in the order.

They were all facing a stone altar, covered with carvings of the moon in various phases, all decorated with gold and precious jewels. A beautiful silk banner hung above the altar.

Because Zabastian had been here many times over the centuries, the sanctuary was familiar to him. Now, though, he was seeing it with Luke and Sidney's eyes, marveling at the rich setting.

For them, it was probably like a church, but not a denomination they had never encountered before.

Sidney was ushered to a pew at the front left, a place

of honor in this group. Zabastian walked to the altar, carrying the briefcase. When he opened it and took out the box, an exclamation rose from the priests who had assembled for the ceremony.

Father Delanos held out his hands, and Luke handed over the box. This was a sacred moment, a moment of great importance for the temple.

But it was also a moment of danger for any flesh and blood person who was in the room.

Luke took a step back before the Master placed the box into a special indentation that had been carved into the top of the altar.

He knew what was happening now. The priests of this temple had constructed the box when they decided that their place was in the background, not in the world of men.

The box was a link to the world, and now it was transferring the power it had absorbed to the altar, infusing the Temple of the Moon with the energy that would keep it going for a hundred years or more. If the box had stayed out in the world for much longer, it would have exploded. But here, it transferred its power to the temple.

As everyone watched, the sacred object began to glow with an otherworldly light.

Sidney gasped.

Probably it was finally sinking in that the wooden object they'd been carrying around was far more than she had dreamed possible. It was a conduit, siphoning power from the universe and drawing it to the temple.

As the box gathered power and the connection heated up, a sizzling sound like an electric current came from the altar. In the next moment, sparks flew from the box, enveloping the altar in a shower of fire that looked like it would burn down the room and the temple with it.

Sidney watched as Zabastian stood his ground. He was too close for comfort, as far as Luke was concerned, the heat like a furnace, searing his skin. And in a terrible moment of truth, Luke understood that he was in deep trouble.

No, he screamed inside his head.

But Zabastian had already made a fateful decision for the two of them, and there was no way Luke could stop him.

In that terrible moment, Luke knew what the warrior had been hiding from everyone, including the man who had lent him his body.

The warrior leaped forward, into the shower of sparks, the fire flaming up around him, the heat and darts of energy sending agony to all of Luke's nerve endings. He was being burned alive, even if his flesh still looked normal.

He wanted to scream in pain and anger, but the warrior kept the anguish locked in his throat.

The room around him faded to gray, but he looked for Sidney and found her. She had leaped to her feet. When she started toward him, two of the priests grabbed her arms and held her in place.

At least she would be safe.

Thank God for that.

The thought came from Luke and from the warrior, too.

Luke opened his mouth, and his voice boomed out, filling the sanctuary.

"I will not go back in the box. I will gladly die here rather than suffer that fate again.

Chapter Fifteen

Sidney watched in horror as the fire enveloped Luke so that he looked like a human torch.

"No!" she screamed over and over, even as she tried to shake off the grasping hands that held her firmly in place.

It couldn't be real. It had to be an illusion created by the priests. They wouldn't allow Luke's odyssey to end this way, would they?

But the priests' panicked reactions told her this was no illusion. Chaos broke out in the sanctuary. Some of the men ran for the back of the room, out of her line of vision.

Others ran toward the altar where two of the priests leaped forward and threw themselves on Luke, pulling him from the heart of the fire.

All three of them fell to the stone floor, unmoving.

Fighting free of the hands that held her, Sidney struggled toward Luke. When she knelt beside him, she gasped.

His skin was so charred that he hardly looked human. The other two men weren't as bad because their time in the fire had been much less than Luke's.

The elegant suit he had worn to the temple lay in shreds—sticking to his body.

The box was still spouting fire. Two men dashed past Sidney, carrying a heavy, richly embroidered blanket which they threw over the altar, cutting off the fireworks. Smoke still seeped from the edges of the blanket, but the flames had been quenched.

At the same time, some of the priests joined Sidney on the floor beside the injured men.

First they carried away the two priests who had dared to pull Luke back. Then four more men picked up Luke and hurried out of the room.

Nobody stopped Sidney from trailing behind as they hurried down a flight of stairs to a room on the floor below.

As they laid Luke's ruined body on a narrow bed, she asked God over and over to save his life.

But it looked like it was already too late. He lay still and lifeless. She could smell something like burned charcoal. And when she touched his charred flesh, some of it flaked away. Quickly she drew her hand back, afraid to injure him more.

"Is he dead?" she whispered.

"It depends on how you view life," the priest named Father Delanos answered.

"This isn't a semantic game," she snapped, then wondered how she could be so disrespectful.

"It is not a game. I simply can't give you a definite answer because his life on earth is hanging in the balance," the priest answered in a calm, even tone.

Because she needed to steady herself, she clutched her own hands in front of her body. "You have magic powers. You told me you have lived for a long time. Can't you cure him?"

"Not magic. And I have lived so long because I have not been injured."

"Okay. It's not magic. I don't care what you call it," she answered, hearing the desperation in her voice. "Can you save him?"

"No," he said, his voice low and deep and very sure of the pronouncement. "I can heal the other two men because they were only briefly in the fire. But Luke's body is beyond my skill."

She felt as though the floor had dropped out from under her feet, and she had to steady herself against the bed to keep from falling.

It was hard to hear the priest over the roaring of blood in her ears, but finally his words penetrated her brain.

"But perhaps you can save him."

A spark of hope leaped inside her. But only a spark. If the priest couldn't do anything, what could she do. "How?"

The priest's voice turned grave. "It is dangerous. You might not survive."

"But if I take the chance, he may live?"

"Yes."

There was no question about her answer, not when she and Luke had been through so much together. Not when she understood in this terrible moment how much he meant to her. "What do I have to do?" she asked.

"His spirit is halfway between this world and the next. If you follow him, perhaps you can bring him back."

"What about the warrior? Will I bring him back, too?"

"I do not know," the priest answered, and she heard the deep regret in his voice.

Though she knew she should keep her opinion to herself, she couldn't stop herself from saying, "You punished Zabastian for something he did long ago. He faithfully did your bidding, but I guess being confined in that box and feeling time ticking by for more than a thousand years was more than he could endure. More than anyone could endure."

"Yes. I understand that now," the priest answered in a low voice. Age does not always bring wisdom. Sometimes it takes a fearful event."

"If I find him and Luke, can I tell him that he doesn't have to return to the box?"

"Yes."

"How do I reach them?"

"I can send you to them. To the gateway between life and death."

She sucked in a sharp breath. "The gateway between life and death. And what do I do when I get there?"

"That is the part I can't tell you. What you do will be up to you."

It sounded like an impossible task, but she gave a small nod and whispered, "Okay."

"Lie down," the priest said.

She started to ask where. Then she saw that the narrow bed was wider now, wide enough for two people.

Without asking how that had happened, she kicked off her shoes and eased onto the white sheet, pressing her shoulder lightly against Luke's, afraid to increase the contact or do anything else that would injure his already mangled skin.

"Close your eyes."

When she did as he'd asked, the priest made a gruff sound. "The next part may hurt."

She braced herself for pain, then felt a jolt like a

knife stabbing into her brain as he laid his hands on her forehead.

The bed seemed to drop away from under her, and then she was lost in absolute and complete nothingness.

She was disconnected from her body, disconnected from every one of her senses, and fear clawed at her throat. She wanted to scream, but no sound came out because sound was impossible.

She was nowhere. Nothing. And it had happened in the space of a heartbeat. Only now she didn't even know if her heart was still beating.

What had she done?

Her eyes were wide open, but she couldn't see. She might have been in the cold, dark reaches of outer space. But in space, her body would explode, wouldn't it?

Instead, the only sensation was of a terrifying free fall, as though she'd jumped from a plane, and her parachute had failed to open. Only, to add to her confusion, she felt like she was falling up not down.

Then, off in the distance, she recognized light shining. It might have been the full moon, or something else. She wasn't sure what she saw. She only knew that her salvation depended on reaching that place where there was hope.

Once again, everything changed in the space of a heartbeat. She was no longer out in the cold dark nothingness. Suddenly, her feet touched down on a solid surface. Relief flooded through her. As she looked around to see where she was, she realized she was in an enclosed space, a tunnel with a curved wall. The light she had seen was shining at the end, calling her.

She ached to rush forward, to embrace the light. That was why she had come here, wasn't it?

Or was it? She pressed her hand to her forehead, trying to dispel the confusion swimming in her brain.

Something else. There was something else she needed to remember.

The light pulled at her, sweeping everything else away. But as she started forward, she saw someone ahead of her in the passageway. It was a man walking in the same direction.

She couldn't see him clearly, yet her chest tightened as she hastened to catch up. She kept staring at his back, trying to puzzle out who he was.

And all it once, it came to her.

It was Luke. She recognized Luke's dark head and his broad shoulder.

With a start, she realized that back in the real world, his flesh had been charred. Here, in this place, he was whole again.

And as that thought came to her, she knew why she was in this place.

To bring him back.

How had she forgotten that?

"Luke!"

He stopped short, his shoulders tensing.

"Luke, wait for me."

He spun around, staring at her, his face contorted with a mixture of alarm and sadness. "Sidney, oh Lord Sidney, did I kill you, too?"

"No! That's not what happened. Not at all. I…I came to bring you back where you belong."

She made the mistake of glancing behind him at the light and she felt the pull of the warmth and radiance.

She wanted to go there. "But not yet." She said it out loud to make sure she understood it was true.

"Not yet," she repeated.

But she needed more than words. To reinforce the conviction, she ran forward, clasping Luke in her arms, hugging him to her, focusing on the sensation of his warm, solid body against hers.

He went very still, then murmured. "Let me go. I have to…go to the other side."

She tightened her grip on him. "No. It's not your time yet. This is a mistake."

He raised his head and looked around. "But I'm here. In the tunnel that leads to the afterlife, so it must be my time." Still, even as he spoke, he sounded like he wasn't certain.

"You're not sure because I'm right! Zabastian didn't want to go back into his prison. That's why you're here. It doesn't have anything to do with you. With Luke McMillan."

He looked surprised, as though memory were flooding back.

To reinforce the memory, she kept talking. "You put the box on the altar. And the light show started. And Zabastian jumped into the flames," she said, her voice bitter.

A dark look came over his face, and his fists clenched. "And my body died," Luke finished.

"No! Father Delanos said you weren't dead. He said I could bring you back."

When he opened his mouth to speak, she rushed on. "Luke, I love you. I didn't get a chance to tell you that. Come back with me, and we can live the rest of our lives together."

For a few heartbeats, she thought he was giving her

his agreement. Then he eased away. "Don't say that. It's too late for us."

Her breath had turned shallow, but she kept her voice strong. "You can't order me to change my feelings about you."

"You hardly know me. How can you love me?"

She looked into his eyes. "The same way you love me. For six months we watched each other and wondered. We thought about each other. But neither one of us was brave enough to bridge the gap between us. Then the Poisoned Ones came, and you got me out of their death trap. You kept me alive while you tried to bring the box back to the temple. You could have just left me along the way, but you didn't. Just like I'm not leaving you now."

He pulled away and looked her in the eye. "Not me. This isn't just about Luke McMillan."

"I'm not forgetting about Zabastian. He was a factor, certainly. But the two of you were working together. He couldn't have done it without you. And when we were safe in your friends' house, we had time for the two of us. You made love to me and I found out how I really felt about you. And so did you—about me. Didn't you?" she challenged.

His face contorted. "Zabastian wasn't thinking about the two of us. He was thinking about controlling the uppity woman."

"You're not going to push me away by saying that kind of stuff. That wasn't what Luke McMillan was thinking, was it?"

He swallowed. "No."

"Do you love me?" she demanded.

"Yes."

"I want to hear you say it," she murmured. If this

ended here, she wanted to have that much. "I want to hear the words."

"I love you."

Before she could rejoice, he went on, "But that doesn't change anything. Zabastian is still inside me. He won't go back to the living hell of the box."

"Father Delanos and I talked about that. The Father realizes the punishment was too much for anyone to endure. He says Zabastian doesn't have to go back into solitary confinement."

His expression changed, and she knew that she had been speaking to the warrior as well as to Luke. He had been there all along, inside Luke, taking in the conversation.

"Father Delanos wouldn't lie," he said, his voice gruff. Zabastian's voice. "But it is still too late," he added with grim finality. "The energy blast fused Zabastian and Luke McMillan together. We cannot be separated."

Sidney wanted to scream. Instead she managed to hang on to some shreds of calm as she addressed herself to the warrior. "Zabastian, what if you could live?" she said, emphasizing each word. "What if you could live through Luke? In his world. Experiencing what he does. Like you've been doing. Only Luke would stay in charge?"

She held her breath, waiting for both men to consider that idea.

When they spoke, it was hard to hear them above the rushing of blood in her ears.

"I cannot accept that," Zabastian said.

SIDNEY HAD DARED SO MUCH and come so far. But with those words, her temper snapped, and she screamed at him. "Why not? You're getting a chance to live—not die."

He glared at her. "What if you were in danger? Would you expect me to stay in the background and let you get hurt when I could save you? Or what if Luke needs my advice? What if I know something that he doesn't and he needs the information?"

She breathed out a sigh. "Is that all you're worried about?"

"Not all. But that is the main thing. And it is enough to make what you suggest impossible."

"Why don't you let Luke speak for himself?" Her gaze locked with his, she asked, "Luke, if he came back with you, would you agree to let him take control if you or I were in danger."

He nodded gravely.

"And…would you take advice from him?"

"That's a little harder to swallow. But yeah, I think I could. I've been doing it. And we've learned how to cooperate in a weird sort of way."

"Then come back with me. Both of you. Please."

She saw that he was still hesitating. "Is there still some problem?"

"Father Delanos said he would not put me back in my prison. But you asked the wrong question."

She felt her heart clench.

"You should have asked if he would punish me."

Sidney knit her fingers together, squeezing them tight enough to make her knuckles ache. "Yes. There might be some consequences. But are you telling me that you're willing to kill Luke McMillan because you are afraid?"

"I am not a cowering dung beetle!" he thundered at her.

"Then take the chance on coming back." She stepped

to him, clasping him to her, locking her hands behind his back.

She knew he was strong. Strong enough to break free of her grasp. But as she stood there with her heart pounding, she realized deep in her soul that he wasn't going to yank himself away.

"Thank God," she murmured, pressing her lips against his cheek.

He turned his head, too, and their mouths met.

She made a glad exclamation that was swallowed by his mouth as he began to kiss her with a hunger he didn't hold in check.

As his lips moved over hers and his arms tightened around her, pure and absolute joy surged through her.

But when he lifted his head again, his expression was grave. "Do you happen to know the way back?"

The question hit her with the force of a rock striking her chest. "No," she whispered.

She looked toward the light.

It still tugged at her. But she knew she must walk away from it if she wanted to go home with Luke.

Turning her back on the warmth of that glow, she looked toward the other end of the tunnel where she saw darkness. She had come from that darkness. Returning there seemed like her only option.

The terror of plunging into that nothingness again made her hesitate. But Luke reached down and clasped her hand. It was warm and strong.

"I know how I got here," she whispered. "Will you take a chance on going back that way?"

"Yes."

His hand tightened on hers, steadying her for the leap

into the black abyss. Whatever happened, they were going to do it together.

"Come on, before I lose my nerve," she whispered.

Together they ran down the tunnel, away from the light, toward something she couldn't see or feel or hear.

Then, suddenly, the solid surface under her feet fell away, and she might have screamed if sound could have come from her throat.

She had faced this once. But that didn't make it any easier the second time.

As she hurtled downward, the terror threatened to swallow her whole.

Chapter Sixteen

But this time, Luke's large, warm hand stayed firmly in hers, anchoring her to something outside herself. Something real and positive.

She had told him she loved him, and he had said it too. That made all the difference.

If she could have turned to look at him, she would have. But she wasn't capable of moving, only of holding tight to him with the breath frozen in her lungs.

They fell through the blackness, joined together because that was what the two of them wanted.

Then all at once, she was lying on her back, staring up at a carved medallion on the ceiling.

She turned her head quickly, and her breath caught. Luke was lying beside her. But he didn't look the way he had on the bed the last time she had been here. He looked the way he had in the tunnel, his complexion ruddy, his skin wonderfully healthy, his eyes shining as his gaze locked on her face.

"Thank you, God," she breathed.

He looked like he couldn't quite believe he was back on earth.

"Believe it," she whispered as she reached for him.

He reached for her at the same time, his arms strong and muscular as he pulled her body half on top of his and brought his mouth to hers, kissing her as though he never meant to let her go.

She kissed him back with the same fervor. When they broke apart, they were both breathing hard, and he was staring at her with a look of wonder.

"I'm really back. With you."

"Yes." She reached to stroke his face. "And you're all right. You're not burned."

"Thanks to you," he murmured.

"I couldn't give you up, not when I knew there was a chance of saving you."

He stared at her with sudden insight. "You risked your life to follow me."

She swallowed. "I had to. I had to give the two of us a chance. We had months to reach out to each other, but we never did it—until we were forced to defend the box together. Then I realized we had been meant to be together all along. I couldn't give that up. Not without a fight."

"Yes. We belong together."

He was moving his lips over hers again when a knock sounded at the door, and she felt her cheeks turn pink. Quickly she sat up and smoothed her hand over her hair.

Luke sat up more slowly. "Yes?" he called out.

"May I come in?" Father Delanos asked from the other side of the door.

Luke glanced at Sidney, and she nodded.

"Yes," Luke answered.

When Father Delanos walked into the room, he looked from her to Luke.

"You brought him back to us," the priest said.

"Yes," Sidney murmured.

"You were brave to undertake that mission."

"I had to do it."

He nodded, then turned his head toward the other occupant of the bed. "And now I must speak to you, Zabastian," the priest said, his voice stern.

The warrior's expression turned rigid, and she reached for his hand, holding tight as the priest continued speak.

"You almost took another man's life by jumping into the fire."

Luke's lips firmed, and his chin jutted upward. "I'm sorry for that. But you gave me no choice."

Sidney braced for a further rebuke. But the priest looked sad and abashed. "We made a mistake with Zabastian, and I want to apologize."

She caught her breath in astonishment, then stole a glance at Luke, and he looked as confounded as she felt.

"Zabastian was a loyal warrior," Father Delanos continued. "And we used him for our own purposes. We should have realized that we were asking him to take on more than any soul could endure."

"Yes," Luke whispered, but she sensed both men answering.

"You are free of us. I hope the time you spend with Luke McMillan will be good for you. I hope it will help make up for your long punishment."

"Thank you," Luke whispered. He straightened his shoulders. "What about the Poisoned Ones?"

"They are dead," the priest said.

"You killed them?" Sidney whispered.

"No. The men who sent them to steal the box punished them for their failure."

"Who are they exactly?" she asked, because all this time she'd been wondering who was really trying to kill them.

"Men who are the ancestors of priests who were part of our society. Some of them wanted power, and they tried to take it from us. They were expelled from the temple and went out to live in the world, marrying women who would continue their line. Over the years, they and their descendants have tried to take the power of the box when we have sent it from the temple into the world to regenerate its power. But they have never been successful. Thanks in part to Zabastian. And lucky for us, because they don't understand that if the chest stays too long outside the temple, it will discharge its energy to very bad effect."

Sidney winced, then asked, "What happens now that you don't have Zabastian working for you?"

"We have decided on another method. The younger ones of us will draw straws, and one will volunteer to guard the box. But for no longer than a hundred years."

"Only a hundred years," Sidney murmured.

"Shortening our lives is a small price to pay to keep the box safe. Our order is important to the world. To keeping the peace among the factions of mankind." He smiled. "Or, I guess the way you would say it in this age is humankind."

"Yes." She gave him a questioning look. "Where will you keep the box?"

"It must be in a place where men—people—gather. We will move from city to city. But not yet. It can stay safe here for a decade before we must make other arrangements."

Sidney swallowed. "When Zabastian leaped into the fire—did he disrupt the power of the box?"

"Only a little. He waited until the end."

Beside her, Luke let out the breath he must have been holding. She glanced at him, seeing the relief on his face. Then she turned back to the priest. She knew she was asking a lot of questions, but she also knew this was her only chance to get answers to some of them.

"And when you're in the temple, how do you keep up with what's going on in the outside world?"

"Now we watch your television and listen to your radio. And sometimes we bring other media into the temple."

She nodded.

"You must leave us soon."

Sidney felt a dart of alarm. Since returning from the tunnel, she hadn't been thinking about the outside world. Now she remembered they still had a problem. "What about the police?" she asked.

"I have adjusted their memories. They no longer remember that they were looking for Sidney Weston and Luke McMillan."

"But our friends from 43 Light Street will remember?" Sidney asked.

"You trust them with that knowledge?" the priest asked.

"Yes." Luke answered, and she felt her heart swell. He had been so opposed to trusting the Light Street men and women, and now she realized he had changed his mind.

"Then your friends will remember," Father Delanos

said. He looked from her to Luke. "It is time for you to leave us. The temple will not be in this location for much longer."

"Where will it be?"

"Where it is needed."

She climbed off the bed, and Luke came around to her side, reaching for her hand again. She looked down at her dress and saw that it was smudged with ashes, as was Luke's suit.

The priest led them down the hall to a long room with two doors. "Walk through there," he said.

They followed directions, and when they came out the door at the other end, their clothing was as clean and fresh as when they'd put it on.

"A neat trick," Sidney murmured.

"They have a lot of neat tricks," Luke said.

The priest gave them a broad grin, then led them up the stairs and down the hall toward the front door of the temple.

Several of the priests were waiting near the large wooden doors, including the two men who had pulled Luke from the fire. She was relieved to see they had recovered.

She embraced both of them. And to her surprise, so did Luke.

"Thank you for your bravery," he said.

"We have met you here before. And we have been impressed with your loyalty and your courage. We couldn't leave you in the fire," one of them said, his eyes moist.

Luke looked embarrassed.

Then Father Delanos began speaking. "We want to reward both of you for your service to us." With a smile, he handed the briefcase back to Luke.

"What are you giving us?"

The father's smile widened. Apparently he was feeling pleased with himself, now that the crisis was over. "Something that will be useful out in the world."

"Thank you," Luke said.

Sidney added her thanks. The priest pulled the heavy door open, and she looked out into the ordinary Baltimore street. It had a feeling of unreality. They'd come here at night, but now it was morning again. Her eyes widened as she saw an SUV parked across the street. Thorn Devereaux was sitting behind the wheel. He looked toward the open doorway, then climbed out and raised his hand in greeting.

"He can see us," Sidney whispered.

Father Delanos stared at the lone figure. "He is a man from another place and time. I have heard about him in the temple records."

Thorn didn't approach, but he leaned against the car, staring at them.

"It is time for you to leave," the priest whispered.

"Thank you," Sidney said, turning and embracing him. "Thank you for letting me bring Luke back."

"I am glad it worked out for you," he said, sincerity ringing in his voice.

They walked through the doors and down the steps. When Sidney looked back, the temple was gone.

Thorn walked toward them. "Are you all right?"

"Yes," she answered. "Thank you for being here." She touched his arm. "You could see the temple."

"Yes. I learned how to do that a long time ago."

They climbed into his car and buckled up. When he started off, Luke asked. "Are we going back to that... private hospital?"

"No. We figured you might need some R and R after whatever happened in there."

Luke sighed. "Right."

"So I'm driving you to the Randolph estate. There's a very nice guesthouse where you can decompress. The refrigerator's stocked with food, and the linens on the bed are fresh. You've got a heated pool, a hot tub, and a home gym. And the movie theater has all the latest DVDs. When you're ready, you can tell us about your adventures."

Sidney felt overwhelmed. "Thank you so much," she murmured, then thought of something that had slipped her mind with everything else she'd had to think about. "What about Carl Peterbalm?"

"He believes he was in the hospital being treated for an injury during a robbery."

"Did he really buy that?" Sidney asked.

"It appears so." Thorn made a dismissive sound. "He doesn't know it yet, but he's going to be facing charges for importing stolen property. And of course, when he has to explain what hospital, he's not going to find the place."

She felt her mouth harden. "Too bad for him. He's overdue for a lot of bad news. Even though that means I'm going to be out of a job. There's no way I could go back to that office now."

"I don't think you have to worry about that," Luke muttered.

Her gaze shot to him. While she'd been talking to Thorn, Luke had been looking inside the briefcase. He reached in and pulled out a neat stack of hundred dollar bills.

Her eyes widened as she stared at them.

"That's just one stack," Luke said, his voice hoarse with amazement.

"Where did it come from? Is it…stolen?"

"Over the years, the Moon Priests have made a lot of investments. They're rich," Luke said, only she knew that Zabastian was the one answering the question.

He pulled out a folded piece of paper, read it and handed it to Sidney. "It says there's a million dollars in the briefcase. And half the money is yours."

"What?"

"A million dollars," he said. "I guess he wasn't kidding. They were grateful for our service."

She dragged in a breath and let it out. "How am I going to explain that much money?"

"We can make it look like a grant from the Light Street Foundation," Thorn answered. He laughed. "For a small charitable donation, of course."

"Yes," Sidney answered, still trying to wrap her head around the sudden change in her fortunes.

She looked at Luke. "I can open my own shop."

"Yes."

Thorn spoke to Luke. "And while we're discussing business, Cameron Randolph said he wanted to talk to you about doing some work for Randolph Security. If you'd like the account. We like to use people we know we can trust, and you certainly fit that bill."

Luke looked stunned. "I'd be honored to work with you," he finally answered.

Sidney leaned back, her head spinning, trying to take it all in.

Thorn arrived at the gates of the Randolph estate. He looked over his shoulder and began speaking to Luke, since Sidney had been here before. "Jo O'Malley and Cameron Randolph live here. Cam owns Randolph Security, and Jo owns the Light Street Detective Agency, which is why the two businesses are associated. If you'd like to see them tomorrow or the next day, feel free to call them. Otherwise, they'd love to have you just relax here for a couple of days."

"That's very kind of them. But I don't want to impose. Why…" Sidney fumbled for the right way to ask why Cam and Jo were being so nice to them.

"They're hoping you can give them some information about Carl Peterbalm's operation when you're ready."

Sidney felt her throat clog. "I feel like a jerk working for a crook."

"You didn't know," Thorn said. "Sabrina was getting ready to ask if you'd come in for an interview. Then everything blew up in your face."

Sidney nodded, craning her neck as she took in the guesthouse. It looked as big as a suburban rancher. She'd been to parties at the main house but she'd never been here.

When the car stopped, she and Luke climbed out. She hugged Thorn, then waved good-bye before stepping into the house with Luke.

As soon as the door was closed, he took her in his arms, hugging her to him. "Sidney. Oh Lord, Sidney. I love you so much. I never thought I could end up with a woman like you."

"Believe it," she said, raising her head so that their lips could meet. After a long, frantic kiss, she realized that there was no need for panic. They had all the time in the world to enjoy being alone together, without killers chasing them and without the weight of Zabastian's awful responsibility.

Luke lifted his head and grinned at her, and she knew he'd figured out the same thing.

"We've got a lifetime to love each other. Do you think you can stand being married to me for a hundred years?"

"That long?"

"I don't know for sure."

"But that was a marriage proposal, right?" she clarified.

"Right."

She hugged him tightly, then felt overwhelmed again. She had Luke McMillan—and Zabastian, too, the warrior who had changed her life and Luke's. But she wasn't just thinking about herself and the man in her arms.

"Suddenly I have so much. Not just for us. I can make my mom's life better, too." She looked at Luke. "She's going to love you like the son she never had."

"I hope I don't disappoint her."

"Never. She always wanted me to marry a nice guy and settle down. She's going to appreciate all your good qualities. And bake cookies for you. And tell you all the family stories." She laughed. "Over and over."

Luke looked stunned. "You're giving me more than I ever expected. After such a long time of loneliness."

The words made her conscious again that Zabastian was still with them. Back in the tunnel, when she had asked him to stay in the background, he had resisted that request. She understood why.

He was a part of Luke now, and he always would be. Which was all right, because she knew the warrior had changed Luke in very fundamental ways. She had admired him before and been attracted to him. Now he had hidden qualities that he could draw on for the rest of his life.

She gave him a teasing grin. "So what do you want to do first? Have me teach you how to make hot chocolate?"

"You're going to put me to work in the kitchen?"

"Um hum."

"How about later." He bent to nibble at her ear. "Maybe we can find out what the bedroom looks like before we get into cooking lessons."

"Good idea," she answered, her heart singing as they walked down the hall hand in hand.

* * * * *

*Mills & Boon® Intrigue
brings you a sneak preview of...*

Dani Sinclair's Bodyguard to the Bride.

*Xavier Drake had been on difficult missions
before, but none more challenging than posing
as Zoe Linden's bodyguard, But once he gets his
hands on this pregnant bride will he be able
to face giving her away...*

*Don't miss this thrilling new story, available next
month in Mills & Boon® Intrigue.*

Bodyguard to the Bride

by

Dani Sinclair

Xavier Drake stared at the woman in the full-length bedroom mirror. He hadn't expected her to be so lovely or so delicate-looking. The cream-colored wedding gown with its simple lines fell gracefully to the floor in soft folds. She turned to the side, studying her reflection in profile. A slender hand smoothed the satiny material against her stomach. Brown hair, burnished to a gleaming teak, framed her oval face.

He continued to watch in silence as she lifted the simple veil from the top of her dresser and placed it on her head. All the trite phrases people used to describe a bride flitted through his mind. For the first time, he understood. Those phrases certainly described this bride-to-be. No wonder Wayne had been so taken with this woman.

Her fawn-colored eyes widened in shock as their gazes met in the mirror. Xavier was already moving forward as she started to turn, lips parting.

"Don't scream," he ordered sternly. "I won't hurt you."

He got his hand over her mouth in time. She fought him then, hampered by the dress. Even without that, she wouldn't have had a chance. He was bigger, stronger, well trained in unarmed combat and far more determined. His free arm wrapped around her chest, pinning her right arm against a firm, full breast. Her left hand clawed his where it covered her mouth. She smelled faintly of cinnamon and vanilla.

"Don't make me drug you."

She stilled at the warning, chest heaving, eyes wide with fear in the mirror. He hated that he'd caused such a look, but he had little choice.

"I'm not going to rape you. I'm not going to hurt you at all if I can help it."

She breathed hard and fast through her nose. Her chest rose and fell beneath his arm. Her body was firm and strong, and she was a perfect height for him.

He shook off the thought. "I need you to come with me and we don't have much time. I'm going to let go of your mouth." He held her gaze sternly. "Don't scream. If you scream, I'll have to silence you. Do you understand?"

She gave a jerky nod.

"Do you promise not to scream?"

The nod came again, less jerky. Slowly, he released her mouth, ready to clamp down again if she drew a deep breath. Instead, the breath she drew was shaky. Eyes flashed in anger, still edged by fear.

"You nearly suffocated me! Let me go!"

"I don't think so."

"You said you weren't going to hurt me."

He relaxed his grip fractionally. "I'm not hurting you."

"My bruises say otherwise. How did you get in here?"

Someone must have told her a strong offense was the best defense. She was scared to death, but she had guts.

"Does it matter?"

Her eyes narrowed. "Harrison said you would stay outside."

"What?"

Still shaken, but now looking more annoyed than scared,

she shook her head. "Let me go. I'm sure Harrison didn't tell you to manhandle me."

He had no idea what she was talking about, but he was relieved and more than a little surprised that she was calm.

"I'll let you go as soon as I'm sure you aren't going to do anything stupid."

Her glare deepened. "Define *stupid.*"

His lips twitched. "Screaming, running, trying to hit me with something."

"Deal."

He released her slowly. Immediately, she crossed to the nightstand. His hand closed over the telephone a moment before hers. "You agreed," he scolded.

"You didn't say anything about making a phone call. I want to talk to Harrison."

"Chew on him later. The others could show up any minute now."

"What others?"

"The men who killed Wayne know where you are. I saw one of them downstairs."

Her lips parted on a soft *oh* of comprehension. Her hand went to her stomach as fear widened her eyes once more. They were very pretty eyes.

"You saw one of them?"

"He was in the parking lot."

"It could have been someone who lives here."

"Or a thief looking for an unlocked car. You willing to take that chance?" Glancing around the room, he spotted a suitcase on the floor near the bed. "Is that case packed?"

"Mostly, yes. I still have a few more things in the dryer."

"Replace them later. Let's go."

"Like this? You're insane. I have to change!"

"Forget it. We don't have time. Consider this a formal kidnapping."

"But—"

"No *buts*. Lady, we have to go now. Every second you delay is costing precious time."

"The name is Zoe."

"I don't care if it's Fred." He grabbed the bag, wondering if it could possibly be this easy. Would she come with him willingly? "Let's go."

"At least let me change my shoes!"

There isn't time died unspoken. She was already stepping out of a pair of sexy slim high heels and sliding her feet into a pair of flat shoes on the floor nearby.

"I am not going to run around anywhere in those high heels. They pinch."

"Then why wear them?"

"They go with my gown. Are you sure there isn't time to change out of this dress?"

"Positive." He had to get her away before trouble really did come knocking or before she started asking more pointed questions—like how she could be sure he'd been sent by this Harrison person, who he assumed was probably the groom.

She snatched the wedding veil from her head, grabbed her purse from the foot of the bed and started down the hall to the living room. He followed, hefting a suitcase that weighed more than it should have given its size, amazed and relieved by this unexpected boon.

"The front door's still locked." A trace of fear returned to her voice as she flipped the dead bolt and looked back at him. "How *did* you get in here?"

He inclined his head toward the sliding glass doors. "The balcony."

"We're three floors up!"

"I know." He reached past her and opened the door. "Take the stairs. We'll go out the back."

"But—"

"Will you be quiet and move!"

She bit back something that no doubt would have singed his ears and stepped into the quiet hallway. Without further prompting, she headed for the stairwell. The fire door opened a second before they reached it. Two men started to step into the hall and stopped dead to stare at them. He shoved the woman behind him without glancing at her.

"Run!"

In slow motion, the larger one fumbled for a gun. Xavier slammed the suitcase into the wiry man in front. He staggered back, jostling the bigger one. The gun dropped from his hand. Xavier followed with a hard shove at the forward man's chest before either of them could go for the dropped weapon. Both men fell back onto the concrete landing.

Using the suitcase, Xavier slammed into the first man with all his strength and aimed a hard kick at his chest. The man fell back against his companion and both men tumbled down the concrete stairs. Spinning, Xavier opened the landing door that had closed at his back and ran down the hall toward Zoe.

The elevator came to a stop and the door slid open. With the skirt of her wedding gown bunched in her hand, Zoe held the door ajar, waiting. An older man started to step outside his apartment.

"Get back!" she yelled to him. "They have guns!"

The elderly man took in Xavier running down the hall with the suitcase, Zoe in her wedding dress and the gun on the carpeting behind him. Without a sound he darted back inside, slamming his door shut.

"Go!" Xavier ordered.

Footsteps pounded down the hall toward them. The elevator doors closed and Xavier pressed the button for Two.

"What are you doing?"

"Hoping they're dumb enough to run to the first floor."

"We'll be trapped!"

"Know anyone on Two?"

"Yes, but we can't put anyone else in danger."

He hit the button for One. "Think you can climb in that dress?"

"You have to be kidding. I'm getting married tomorrow. I can't get this dress dirty."

"If they kill you before morning, you won't have to worry about it, lady."

"I told you, the name is Zoe."

"Right." The door opened on Two. He stuck out his head. The sound of footsteps running down the concrete stairs was audible even from there. "Which apartment?"

"What?"

"Which apartment? You said you know people."

"227. Down the hall around the corner, but—"

"No *buts*, remember?"

Grabbing her hand, he tugged her in his wake. There was no sound from inside apartment 227 even after he rapped hard on the door.

"They probably aren't home," she told him breathlessly. "It's a Friday night."

"Good. Let's hope their dead bolt is as cheap as yours." Stepping back, he aimed a kick at the panel beside the doorknob.

"What are you doing?"

"Saving our lives." Three kicks and the door sprang open. Zoe gasped. Xavier hauled her inside and shut the broken door. "They'll need a new lock."

"Are you crazy?"

"Those men have guns," he reminded her.

"Don't you?"

"No." He scanned the dark interior, tugging her toward the balcony.

"What kind of bodyguard doesn't carry a gun?"

"The kind trying to save your life. Come on."

"What are you doing?"

"It isn't going to take them long to figure out where we went," he warned as he opened the balcony door. "Hopefully, right now that old man or one of your other neighbors is calling the police."

"I am not climbing off a second-story balcony," she panted.

He eyed her dress. "Yeah. Might be a stretch. I'll lower you."

Her hands went to her stomach. "No!"

Tossing her suitcase to the ground and grateful it didn't open and spill what had to be half the contents of her apartment, he grabbed her around the waist before she realized what he was going to do.

"No! Stop! I'll get hurt! I'll break something!"

"Make it your arm," he told her as he swung her, kicking and struggling over the railing. "You're going to need your legs to run."

"No!"

Xavier ignored her, lowering her as far down as he could. "Head for the parking lot. Don't stop and don't look back."

She shrieked as he let her go.

© Patricia A Gagne 2008

INTRIGUE

Coming next month

2-IN-1 ANTHOLOGY

COLTON'S SECRET SERVICE by Marie Ferrarella

Undercover agent Nick needs to concentrate on protecting a senator. Yet beautiful distraction Georgie Colton has other things in mind!

RANCHER'S REDEMPTION by Beth Cornelison

Thrown into the path of danger, red-hot rancher Clay must work with his ex-wife to uncover secrets about a crime as well as their true feelings for each other.

2-IN-1 ANTHOLOGY

THE HEART OF BRODY McQUADE by Mallory Kane

People said that no woman would find her way into tall, dark cop Brody McQuade's heart. Could Victoria prove them wrong?

KILLER AFFAIR by Cindy Dees

When Maddie and Tom's plane crashes on a remote island they're suddenly at the mercy of a killer. Can rugged Tom keep Maddie alive *and* win her heart?

SINGLE TITLE

DARK LIES by Vivi Anna
Nocturne

The last thing werewolf Jace wants to do is partner up with human police escort Tala. But she has a dark secret that could bind them together forever...

On sale 17th July 2009

Available at WHSmith, Tesco, ASDA, Eason and all good bookshops.
For full Mills & Boon range including eBooks visit
www.millsandboon.co.uk

INTRIGUE

Coming next month

2-IN-1 ANTHOLOGY

SHEIKH PROTECTOR by Dana Marton

Karim was the most honourable sheikh and fiercest warrior throughout the kingdom. He vowed to protect Julia and her unborn child, but he didn't bank on falling in love!

SCIONS: REVELATION by Patrice Michelle
Nocturne

When Emma's aunt is captured, she must join forces with mysterious yet sexy Caine to set the worlds of the vampires, werewolves and panthers on their true paths.

SINGLE TITLE

LOADED by Joanna Wayne

Oil tycoon Matt Collingsworth couldn't abide his name being dragged through the mud. But for determined CIA agent Shelley he was willing to get dirty!

SINGLE TITLE

BODYGUARD TO THE BRIDE by Dani Sinclair

Posing as Zoe's bodyguard was Xavier's most challenging mission yet. And once he got his hands on the pregnant bride it would be impossible to give her away!

On sale 7th August 2009

Available at WHSmith, Tesco, ASDA, Eason and all good bookshops.
For full Mills & Boon range including eBooks visit
www.millsandboon.co.uk

2 FREE

BOOKS AND A SURPRISE GIFT!

We would like to take this opportunity to thank you for reading this Mills & Boon® book by offering you the chance to take TWO more specially selected titles from the Intrigue series absolutely FREE! We're also making this offer to introduce you to the benefits of the Mills & Boon® Book Club™—

- ★ FREE home delivery
- ★ FREE gifts and competitions
- ★ FREE monthly Newsletter
- ★ Exclusive Mills & Boon Book Club offers
- ★ Books available before they're in the shops

Accepting these FREE books and gift places you under no obligation to buy, you may cancel at any time, even after receiving your free shipment. Simply complete your details below and return the entire page to the address below. You don't even need a stamp!

YES! Please send me 2 free Intrigue books and a surprise gift. I understand that unless you hear from me, I will receive 4 superb new titles every month for just £3.19 each, postage and packing free. I am under no obligation to purchase any books and may cancel my subscription at any time. The free books and gift will be mine to keep in any case.

19ZED

Ms/Mrs/Miss/Mr ....Initials ....
BLOCK CAPITALS PLEASE

Surname ....

Address ....

....

....Postcode..............................

Send this whole page to:
UK: FREEPOST CN81, Croydon, CR9 3WZ